Pigeon Problems

An Urban Bird Researcher's Journal

Book design by Jake Slavik
Illustrations by Arpad Olbey

Design Elements: Shutterstock Images and iStockphoto

Published in the United States by Jolly Fish Press, an imprint of North Star Editions, Inc.

First Edition
First Printing, 2018

This is a work of fiction. Names, characters, places, and incidents are either the product of the author's imagination or are used fictitiously, and any resemblance to actual persons living or dead, business establishments, events, or locales is entirely coincidental.

Library of Congress Cataloging-in-Publication Data (pending)
978-1-63163-188-7 (paperback)
978-1-63163-187-0 (hardcover)

Jolly Fish Press
North Star Editions, Inc.
2297 Waters Drive
Mendota Heights, MN 55120
www.jollyfishpress.com

Printed in the United States of America

Pigeon Problems

An Urban Bird Researcher's Journal

by J. A. Watson

Illustrations by Arpad Olbey | Text by Jodie Mangor

JOLLY
FiSH
PRESS

Mendota Heights, Minnesota

A Crazy Decision

Dear Journal,

Today, I did something I seriously hope I don't regret. I, Anthony Briggs, joined the Science Squad. It's a club that does citizen science, which means we're going to help real scientists answer real research questions. Along the way, we complete projects and earn badges that allow us to level up, video-game style.

My first project is earning the Data Collection badge. And here's the part that just about made me fall off my seat: Anyone who earns this badge moves up to the orange level AND gets to go on a museum overnight! Imagine, an entire night at the Museum of Natural History. Talk about serious inspiration for my comics—that museum has one of the greatest dinosaur collections in the world. Barosaurus, Allosaurus, Stegosaurus, you name it. They even have a dinosaur mummy! Not to mention that you get to wander around with the whole place to yourself, in the dark, with flashlights. Nothing can beat it!

Cool, right?

It would be, except . . .

Wait for it . . .

Our group will be studying pigeons. Yup, that's right, garbage-eating rat-birds.

Why do I hate pigeons? First, there's no getting away from them. No matter where you go, they're all around the city, lurking on top of lampposts, sitting on window ledges, and hanging around the garbage cans looking for handouts. The guy who wrote the children's book *Don't Let the Pigeon Drive the Bus* had it right. His pigeon character is nonstop pushy. We New Yorkers have a rep for being pushy, but we're nothing compared to New York pigeons.

Second, pigeons and me have an ugly history that dates all the way back to fifth grade. That was a tough year. As if TJ, the class bully, weren't mean enough, he had to keep saying that I walk like a pigeon and calling me "Pidge" nonstop. It's not like I could help that my walk got all stiff and funny. I'd like to see HIM handle the pain of having his shin bones grow way too

6

fast. What would he do if HIS legs started to bow out because HE had something called Blount's disease?

Pidge this, Pidge that. I wanted to punch him so bad. (I still do.) But I was a lot smaller than him (I still am), so I just ignored the comments. TJ has a rep for forgetting his homework, gym shorts, lunch, you name it, so I figured he'd forget about the stupid nickname too.

And he might have, if it weren't for The School Yard Incident. Which is reason number three. Hold on, I need some creepy music—the soundtrack from *Jaws*—to get me in the mood to write about this.

Okay, ready.

There I was, on the playground. An innocent little fifth grader patiently waiting for his favorite swing to open up. Without warning, something hit my shoulder. It was small, but still hard enough to sting. At first, I thought someone had chucked a pebble at me. I whipped around, but everyone was busy doing their own thing, basketball and games of Pokémon.

Then I looked up. There they were, lined up on the monkey bar platform right above me: a fleet of pigeon bombers. Every so often, one of them released a small missile of pigeon poop. *FFFFwwweeeeeeee, plop!* THAT'S what had landed on my shoulder. The evidence was there, white and watery against my dark-blue hoodie.

Ivy and Erica, the two swing hogs, saw it go down. Which means that pretty soon the whole class knew about it. Everyone had a good laugh, even Jasmine, who usually sticks up for me.

I was smiling along with everyone else. "Ha ha, yeah, look at my sweatshirt." I acted like I didn't care. But when I pulled the sweatshirt off, some of the pigeon poo smeared onto my hair and cheek! In that moment, I learned an important truth: Pigeons are evil—and they're out to get me.

Seriously.

Here's another important truth: Poop can be a grossly funny thing, as long as it's not on you. Then it's just plain gross.

That was last year. I've made a mental note to NEVER stand near the monkey bars again. But my whole class STILL calls me Pidge. The fact that I have leg braces (which help with my walk) now makes no difference. I pretend it doesn't bother me. Ha. If I could vaporize all the silly, stupid pigeons in New York, I would. Poof! Gone in a cloud of feathers, never to return.

Today, Mr. Mitts used up half of our science class to tell us about the Science Squad. When he got to the part about how we could sign up and earn the chance to go on a museum overnight, I had to weigh which was stronger: my love for nighttime adventure or my hate for pigeons. By the time Ivy passed the signup paper to me, I had made up my mind. I snatched the sheet out of her hand. It was already almost full with names—Erica, Ivy, Neeko, Jasmine, Pablo, and more. Everyone is going to go after that overnight prize!

I wrote my name in all caps on the last free line.

I seriously hope I don't regret it.

For Anthony's Eyes Only!!!

Top-secret comic book idea: Dino Tech Destroyers

Synopsis: A wormhole opens up between Earth and a parallel world filled with super-smart, highly evolved talking dinosaurs. When the meat-eating dinos enter our world, they fall in love with our technology. Siri, Fitbits, night-vision goggles, and super large flat screens—it's all new and awesome to them. They hatch a plan to take over Earth and turn it into a tech production center for stuff they can take back to their own world.

Meanwhile, the plant-eating dinos want to keep their own world the way it is—after they unload all the nasty meat-eaters on Earth.

But the humans have their own plan. They plan to take over the dino world since it is much fresher and cleaner than Earth. But first they need to avoid being eaten or enslaved by the meat-eaters. They also have to get around the mind games of the plant-eaters.

There will be lots of battles as everyone fights for what they want. Sometimes the humans and plant-eaters will team up against the meat-eaters, while secretly plotting against each other.

This could be the next big Marvel hit!

I'm not telling anyone, not even Jasmine, at least not until I have some of the pages done. I do not want anyone scooping my idea.

More Reasons
Why I Hate Pigeons

What is it with everyone? Mr. Mitts spent the entire class talking about pigeons! I was ready to make earplugs out of erasers. Mr. Mitts told us that people started keeping Rock Pigeons—the kind we have here in NYC—thousands of years ago all over Africa, Asia, Europe, and the Middle East.

Notice how America is not on that list. There were no Rock Pigeons here until the 1600s. Then some wise guys from Europe had the bad idea of bringing pigeons to Canada to use in pot pies. Some escaped, and the rest is history.

Our continent could have been forever pigeon-free if it weren't for pigeon pot pies. I was so annoyed that Erica had to step on my foot to get my attention. She handed me a note, and one look at the hot-pink glitter ink told me Ivy wrote it. It said: "Everyone ask Mr. Mitts a question. If we can keep him talking until the bell, he won't have a chance to check homework! Pass it on."

When Mr. Mitts looked left, I passed the note to Pablo, but no way was I raising my hand. Anything I said in front of the class would be fuel for TJ to make fun of me. Plus, my homework was done. But I could tell whose wasn't by the hands that went up.

Mr. Mitts looked really pleased to see kids raising hands. He's so easy to trick. Here's how it went down:

Ivy: "How many pigeons are there here in New York City?"

Mr. Mitts: "I've heard at least eighty thousand, but I personally think there's a whole lot more."

Ivy: "Whoa—that's one pigeon for every one hundred people!"

Mr. Mitts: "Always quick with the math, Ms. Trimble."

Neeko (into an imaginary microphone, which he then held out to Mr. Mitts): "What do YOU think about pigeons, Mr. Mitts?"

The pigeons that live in New York City and many other cities around the world are Rock Pigeons, or Rock Doves. Their scientific name is *Columba livia*. The windowsills and ledges of buildings and bridges are similar to the rocky cliffs where they once lived in the wild. Rock Pigeons have few natural predators in the city: mainly falcons, hawks, and people who want to get rid of them.

Mr. Mitts: "Well, some people want them all to be exterminated, but I personally like them. They're really smart and have done a lot of good things for people."

Neeko: "Like what?"

Mr. Mitts: "Well . . . they served as messengers during World War I. Have you heard of Mon Cheri? No? He was a famous pigeon who flew through enemy fire. One of his legs was shot off, and he was blinded in one eye, but he still managed to deliver his message, and it saved the lives of two hundred American soldiers."

Neeko: "For real?"

Mr. Mitts: "If you ever go to the Smithsonian Museum in our fine capital city of Washington, DC, you can see for yourself. His stuffed body and the message he delivered are on display there."

Okay, the little pigeon deserves *some* credit.

And now for the bad part.

TJ (looking right at me): "How much poop do pigeons cover the city in each year?"

Neeko and some of the other kids snickered, but Mr. Mitts didn't miss a beat. He said a single bird makes twenty-five pounds of droppings a year. And that historically, people valued pigeon guano (a fancy name for poop) as a great fertilizer, so much that they hired armed guards to protect their dovecotes (a fancy name for pigeon hotels). Blah-blah-blabbity-blah blah blah. Who knew there was so much to say about it?

TJ: "So when Anthony got pooped on, it was like someone passing him a hundred-dollar bill?"

Everyone laughed. Ha ha. I pulled the hood of my sweatshirt up and looked over my already-done homework, pretending I didn't hear. Instead, I worked on an idea for a Dino Tech Destroyers comic scene:

An evil human (who looks *a lot* like TJ) is busy taunting a good guy (who is small like me) for helping the plant-eaters save their world. But little does he realize that he's standing right underneath an Apatosaurus. As he talks, the Apatosaurus unleashes a gigantic dino-load right over his head.

No matter how many times he washes up, ~~TJ~~ the evil guy never smells quite the same again.

Cold Feet

I'm sitting in study hall, yawning nonstop. The desktop is looking pillow soft, but if I let my head sink into it, Ms. Neeling will chuck a piece of chalk at my head. Maybe writing in this journal will help keep me awake.

This morning, Mom asked why I looked so tired. I told her that The Mouth's snoring had kept me awake. My brother may be a quiet guy when he's awake, but his snores are so loud, they make the walls shake! The room he and I share is small and stuffy, but if I open the window, all the street noise pours in: sirens, bachata, hip-hop music, and people talking and yelling. Plus, the ache under my knees has been amping up at night. I've been keeping that last part to myself, though, because I don't want to make Mom's forehead wrinkle.

Mom says I should call my brother by his name, Sammy. The thing is, he *likes* being called The Mouth. All his high school friends call him that. They all have names they've made up for each other: Big E, Slackjaw, and UGee. Their nicknames mean they're part of a brotherhood—the opposite of Pidge, which leaves me stuck alone on the outside.

Speaking of which, the first Science Squad meeting is today after school, and I've got cold feet. What if TJ is on the Squad? I don't remember seeing his name on the signup sheet, but then again, I was so excited I hadn't remembered to look for it.

Jasmine stopped over last night. One advantage of living in the same building is that we can stop by each other's apartments whenever we want. Actually, it's usually Jasmine coming to see me—I'm more likely to text. Also, I think she likes being able to get away from Little Lou (her three-year-old sister) every so often.

When I told Jasmine I wasn't going to be part of the Squad if TJ joined, she got in my face about it. She said I shouldn't give him any power over me, and who cares if he acts like a jerk and calls me names? Why let it get to me? She also threatened to find me and drag me to the meeting if I didn't show. And she would too!

Jasmine has a point. Last year, I skipped the end-of-year swim party. I love swimming. But I can't swim with my leg braces on. I would have had to walk around *the pool with them off, and my walk was way worse then than it is now. So while all the other kids got to dive into the cool, refreshing water, I sat at home in my hot apartment, sweating and regretting.*

Everyone talked about the party all summer. Especially how Neeko jumped in with all his fake gold bling, and the chlorine made it (and his neck and stomach) turn green. I ended up wishing I had gone. And here I am doing almost the same thing again.

"Little dude," my brother's said to me more than once, "You gotta stop thinking about other people so much. I guarantee you they don't spend all that time thinking about you."

He doesn't say much, but when he does, it's usually worth listening to.

He and Jasmine are right. No way am I going to give up my chance at the museum overnight.

That's it. Science Squad, here I come!

Science Squad Meeting #1

We had the first Science Squad meeting today after school. I got there nice and early. I like being early. That way, I don't have to deal with other kids watching me walk across the room.

I sat down and kept my fingers crossed as the other kids trickled in. I seriously hoped TJ wouldn't walk through the door. Jasmine came in and sat next to me. She had on her favorite T-shirt, the one with pictures of birds from all over the world. There are some really crazy looking ones, like spoonbills, toucans, and (my favorite) the frogmouth bird. It's got an ugly-cute thing going on. Jasmine loves every animal there is. Warthogs, pigeons, tarantulas—as long as it's alive, she'll have something nice to say about it. Like the time we found a bunch of larvae wiggling on an unidentified object on the sidewalk. I gagged. She said, "They're cleaning up the mess. Who else would be so brave?"

Jas asked me if we were going to walk home together. I don't know why she bothers, since we always do. Then Ivy and Erica came over, and Jas started whispering and giggling with them. I couldn't hear what they were saying, but that didn't bother me. Jasmine and I go way back to when we were both in diapers and Mom used to watch us while Jasmine's mom worked. That was before Dad took off and Mom had to work all the time. Pros: Jasmine and I are tight and have each other's backs. Cons: My mom has pictures of Jas and me wearing diapers and drooling over chew toys. Sometimes she'll take them out, tear up, and murmur, "Aren't these babies just the cutest thing?" So embarrassing. That's my cue to leave the room.

At four o'clock, it was time for the meeting to start, and there was still no sign of TJ. A young woman carrying a big crate with a box full of papers balanced on top bustled in. She plunked it down and smiled at us. "Welcome to Project Pigeon Power! I'm Miss Diesha. I'll be heading this citizen science project," she said. "Thanks so much for volunteering your time."

I was so surprised that she was the scientist, I made a funny noise in my throat. All the girls giggled, and Jasmine elbowed me. But Miss Diesha just kept on smiling, friendly as could be. She doesn't look anything like the way I think of scientists. She's got four thick braids that are crazy-long and have purple tips! And she has purple fingernails to match. She could be a fashion model. But when she started talking, I could tell she has a passion for science.

She said that Project Pigeon Power could not happen without hundreds of citizen scientists like us. We volunteers make it possible to ask big questions that need lots of data.

Excellent!

But some of the other stuff she said was harder to swallow. Like that the project would be easy and fun, and that she hoped we'd come to love pigeons as much as she did. Another funny noise squeaked out of me. The girls giggled again. I clamped my hand over my mouth to keep it from happening again.

Miss Diesha said pigeons were her passion. And to prove it, she opened up the crate and pulled out a real, live pigeon. It was dingy gray with beady, red eyes. Ugh! Then she invited us to take a closer look.

I hung back, thinking this Science Squad thing was a big mistake. What's she going to have us do? Groom pigeons? Clip their nails? Count their feathers? No way will I ever touch one. I've heard that pigeons are disease factories.

Neeko must not have known this, because he asked to hold the pigeon. Miss Diesha passed it to him. I was surprised by how gently he took it. He'll slam into other basketball players on the court. But apparently pigeons turn him into mush. He even talked baby talk to it, right in front of everyone! The pigeon made cooing noises back. So embarrassing! It was like they were in love or something. I'll be counting the days to see how long it takes for him to get some nasty pigeon disease.

Miss Diesha said she'd tell us the details of Project Pigeon Power and how to earn the Data Collection badge next week. In the meantime, she wants us to find out all we can about pigeons. "Background research," she called it. We're supposed to find a good pigeon-watching place that we can easily get to. And we're also supposed to test "our powers of observation," since great scientists are curious and pay attention to everything, even the details that no one else bothers with.

At the end of the meeting, we took the Science Squad Oath. Here it is:

"I promise to follow the scientific process, make thoughtful, data-based conclusions, respect the Earth and all its creatures, and always stay curious."

(Under my breath, I added, "except for when it comes to pigeons!")

So there it is. I'm officially a member of the Science Squad.

What Jas and I Talked about on Our Walk Home

Jasmine: "This is going to be so great. I mean, I see pigeons all the time, but I never really thought about what they do."

Me: "I wish we were studying squirrels or sparrows. Pigeons are gross and dirty, and they mess up the city. It sounds like a waste."

Jasmine: "Nuh-uh! They're birds, and all birds are amazing. (Points to shirt.) Besides, pigeons are really smart. They're like the geniuses of the bird world."

Me: "I thought crows were the smart ones. They use tools, right? I don't see pigeons doing anything like that."

Jasmine: "But they're great problem solvers. And they're super good at picking out patterns—they can even recognize all the letters of the alphabet and learn to pick out real four-letter words from ones that are made up."

Me: "What!? No way. You made that up."

Jasmine (eye roll): "Did not! It was in the newspaper."

That made me think of some nice four-letter words I'd like to use on pigeons, but I knew it would make Jasmine mad, so I kept it to myself.

Me: "Crazy. But I still hate them. If touching pigeons is part of this project, I'm quitting!"

Jasmine: (another eye roll)

Rat-birds aside, we both agreed that Miss Diesha is good at getting people pumped up. After listening to her, we felt like we could go out and discover the next big thing in science, just by paying attention.

As we walked, a big bird swooped overhead. It moved so fast I almost missed it.

Jas caught a glimpse of it too. She said it was a bird of prey—a hawk or a falcon. Since when have we had birds like that in the city? And why can't we study them?

Jas and I quizzed each other on our observation skills. We tried to remember what Mr. Mitts was wearing today at school, which is easy since the guy only has one set of clothes: a blue button-down shirt and a smiley-face tie. I sure hope he has more underwear than shirts. And what does he wear when he has to do laundry?

Then we went through our family members. I tried to think of what my mom had on this morning. I couldn't, except for the big hoop earrings she always wears, so that doesn't count. The Mouth was easier. I remembered his red boxers because his jeans were slung so low that I thought he was going to lose them.

Jasmine couldn't think of what her mom or Little Lou had on. She said it's hard enough figuring out what to wear herself!

We both decided we need to be more observant. We made a pact to pay better attention to the things around us, including little everyday stuff, like what's sitting on the kitchen counter or who we pass on the sidewalk.

Before heading off to our separate homes, I asked Jasmine to meet me at the park near our building later to see if it would work as a pigeon-watching place, but she had dance class. So I told her I'd check it out for both of us.

The Homefront

When I told Mom about the Science Squad, she overreacted as usual. She clapped her hands and hugged me. "Our baby is going to be a scientist!" I wish she'd stop with the "our baby."

Mr. Geo was there, and he patted me on the back. He likes to act fatherly even though the way I see it, he's just a neighbor who likes to hang around—too much, in my opinion. Then he launched into how smart pigeons actually are (he sounded a lot like Jasmine) and how he thinks they recognize the different groundskeepers at the building where he works. They all hang around the one guy who feeds them. Note to self: Never feed a pigeon.

Ever since we found out I have the leg problem (aka Blount's disease), Mom tries to be extra encouraging. That is, when she's not exhausted from working all day at the restaurant. I know she's trying, but it doesn't always feel real. Like, if she leans in over a drawing that isn't coming out the way I want it to, she'll act like it's amazing and should be hanging in the Museum of Modern Art. But really, I know the only place it should be is inside a garbage truck. Sometimes I'll crumple the paper up and throw it at the wall, just to show her how wrong she is.

There are times when I can hear her talking on the phone, worrying about me to a friend. But to my face, she acts all bright and cheerful. I know it's because she doesn't want me to stress, but I end up feeling like I have to pretend that everything is okay too, even when it isn't. I wish I hadn't mentioned the Science Squad, because now she'll be asking about it all the time. Sometimes I just want some space to do things on my own, to make art without anyone looking over my shoulder, to worry about my legs if I want to, or to just chill without Mom checking on who I'm texting.

Luckily, The Mouth gets me. At least I think he does—he really doesn't say much. Ever. But he gives me space and listens when I need him to. Today, I told him that even if the project stinks, Miss Diesha seems pretty interesting. He said he'd help me scope out some pigeon-watching places tomorrow. Then, it being Friday night, he disappeared into the bathroom for *two hours* to get ready to hang out with his friends. Sometimes I'm tempted to set up a spy cam to find out exactly what it is he does in there for so long. But I probably don't want to know.

Me, I'm going to put on some hip-hop (the clean versions so Mom doesn't come and break down my door) and work on making characters for my comic!

Pterodactyl

Ankylosaurus

Out with
The Mouth

I like being with The Mouth because with him by my side, no one will mess with me. He knows everyone in our hood.

"Hey, Sammy," the two old men sitting in front of the bodega called out as we walked up. They sit there just about every day, telling each other stories in rapid-fire Spanish while sipping from bottles of red and green Mexican soda. I'm too shy to ever say anything to them, but since The Mouth comes in here all the time to pick up rice, dried beans, onions, and other stuff for Mom, he's gotten to know them.

Inside the bodega, the woman behind the counter smiled and handed him a can of cola. Then she whipped up three tacos for him. Just like that, without him even having to order. I guess he's what you'd call a regular. With all the time he already spends at home eating, plus all that food Mom brings home from the restaurant,

I wonder how he finds the time—or the room in his stomach—to come down here to eat even more.

Back on the sidewalk, we passed a couple of kids from The Mouth's high school. They punched him on the shoulder, and he grinned and nodded. Someday, I want people on the street to notice me *like that.*

When we got to the park, we didn't see any pigeons. It was a nice fall day. Pretty warm, but no pigeons. Where the heck were they all? The one time I actually wanted *to see them, and there were none in sight.*

I was ready to take off, but The Mouth put his hand on my knee and said, "Chill." So I whipped out this notebook and started writing. He whipped out his tacos and started eating. Just like that, a bunch of pigeons suddenly appeared. The Mouth gave me a knowing look and grinned. It hit me: Pigeons know to come where people are eating. Maybe they are *smart!*

The Mouth didn't drop much from his taco, but when he did, a pigeon would dart in and grab it. We sat and watched the pigeons strut their stuff. More and more kept showing up, like it was a party. I guess they like to hang out in groups just like people.

That was an observation. It made me think of what Miss Diesha told us about the Data Collection badge. To get it, we have to earn these four different types of stickers, which will show up on our profile pages on the Science Squad website:

- **Observation:** *We earn this first sticker by being curious and observant.*
- **Knowledge:** *To get this one, we'll need to know, in detail, what pigeons look like, how they act, and why. Kind of like that old Chinese quote, "to know your enemy, you must become your enemy," but in this case we become the pigeon. (Ain't gonna happen!)*
- **Fieldwork:** *Don't let the name of this sticker fool you—it has nothing to do with being a farmhand or working in an actual field. Miss Diesha says that for scientists, "fieldwork" means collecting data out in the real world (as opposed to in a lab). So this sticker has to do with collecting data on pigeons.*
- **Engagement:** *To earn this sticker, Miss Diesha says we'll have to "take it one step beyond." What the heck is that supposed to mean? I'd ask Miss Diesha, but she made it clear that we have to figure this out ourselves.*

Once we've earned all four stickers, the Data Collection badge will appear on our profiles too. We'll also get to move up from the red level to the orange level. Miss Diesha said the first two stickers are pretty easy to earn, to hook us in and give us a taste of success. The second two will be a lot harder. It sounds like a lot of work, but it'll be worth it, especially when we finally get to go on the museum overnight.

Since I was at the park, I decided I might as well start on the observation sticker. This is what I noticed:

- Pigeons are ugly.
- They must give themselves headaches by bobbing their heads back and forth. Why do they do that?
- Pigeons have red eyes. This must mean they are devilish.
- Their legs are red. (See? Devilish!)
- Their feathers come in different colors and patterns. Some have shiny, rainbow neck feathers that are kind of cool.

I also spent some time people watching. A grumpy old man sat on the bench closest to us. He was reading a big, thick book, but every once in a while, he'd look up. I think he was checking me out too. With his crooked nose and combed-back hair, he looked like an Italian mobster. I imagined him smoking a cigar and counting large piles of money made from illegal gambling. Maybe he's a Boss, and he was sitting there undercover, waiting for his underlings to report on a heist they pulled off . . . or maybe he's just an old guy who likes hanging in the park.

The Mouth let me finish off his cola (it was kind of warm, and I sincerely hope it wasn't all backwash). Then we got up to go. By the time I got home, I had a plan: Go to the park every day and eat a taco or sandwich so the pigeons show up.

Pigeons aren't the only birds that bob their heads when they walk. Chickens, cranes, and magpies do too. Scientists think this motion helps with vision. While bobbing, the bird's head briefly stays still so its eyes can lock onto an image of its surroundings. Then the bird's head darts forward again, and its eyes lock onto something new. In this way, the bird builds a steady visual image of the scene around it. Humans and many other animals accomplish the same thing with slight eye movements.

A "Coo-Coo" Saturday Afternoon

When I got home, a book about pigeons was lying on my bed with a note: *from Mr. Geo.* Huh. If he thinks this is going to make me start to like pigeons, he's wrong. It's a nice thought but a waste of money. I wish he'd bought me comics—I'd much rather have issues of *The Tick* or *The Avengers*.

Who writes a book about pigeons? I flipped it open. A strange-looking bird stared up at me. It had a huge tail like a peacock's and a puffed-up chest. The caption read *Fantail pigeon.*

I turned the page. This time, the photo was of a pigeon with a big puff of feathers where its head should be. The caption said *Jacobin pigeon.* Crazy! Maybe there are eyes and a beak somewhere in there, but I sure couldn't see them. And to make it even weirder, the rest of its body was pretty thin!

These birds were even stranger than the frogmouth bird on Jas's shirt. They reminded me of the time I checked the *Guinness Book of World Records* out from the library. Some of the things (the world's largest bagel, the loudest burp ever, or the fastest ice cream scooper) were fun. But there were enough highly disturbing photos to make me afraid to turn the page. Like the most body piercings—ugh!! Or the world's stretchiest skin. Or the biggest tumor ever. So gross! I will never get that picture out of my mind. The book creeped me out so much that I had to ask The Mouth to bring it back to the library for me.

I wonder what a regular Rock Pigeon would think of these weird pigeon photos. Would they make its stomach twist up the way mine did when I saw the pictures of the giant tumor?

I looked at a few more pages of the pigeon book. One bird looked like its back was covered in lace, which turned out to be weird, curly feathers. Another one had feathers as big as its wings coming out of its feet. Can some of these birds fly? And how do they even exist? I was curious enough to read some of the book. It turns out that humans have bred pigeons for hundreds of years to get interesting colors and characteristics. Even the famous scientist Charles Darwin used to breed pigeons. Back in the mid-1800s, he came up with the theory of evolution, which explains how different kinds of living things change slowly over time to better adapt to their environments so that they (and their babies) can survive. Pigeons interested Darwin because they can take on a lot of different shapes and looks.

Here's one more interesting thing I found in the book: a photo of pigeons gazing into a mirror. The caption said that pigeons can recognize themselves in a mirror. I was thinking, so what? But I read more, and I found out it's a big deal. There are only a few animals that can do this, like great apes, dolphins, humans . . . and pigeons.

Reading about this gave me the urge to check myself out. So I went over to the mirror hanging above my dresser and looked into it. Then my eye caught some pieces of colored paper on my desk, and an idea popped into my head.

I got a long, black sock out my drawer and tied it around my head. Then I slid some of the slips of paper into my headband.

I turned my head to the left and right. In the mirror, they looked and moved kind of like feathers.

I put on some dance music. With my head and neck bobbing in and out, I sang along. Except I replaced all the words with *coo.*

If anyone saw me, they would have thought I was totally cuckoo. Or should I say, *coo-coo.* (Ha! Get it?)

When Mom tapped on my door, I whipped off my headband. No way would I want to be caught like this!

She told me to come set the table. My answer? *Coo.*

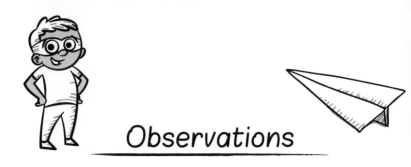

Observations

Today I made a real effort to pay attention to details around me. Who knows? Maybe I'll make a great scientific discovery by noticing something that's been right in front of me all along. Here's a list (Miss Diesha and Mr. Mitts would call these field notes):

- **Neeko:** Drinks two chocolate milks every day, and after lunch, you can see a line of dried milk on his upper lip. He also walks funnier than I do, but in his case, it CAN be helped. All he needs to do is pull up his pants a little.

- **TJ:** Cracks his gum and rolls it around inside his mouth. Sometimes he'll chew his gum and eat a snack at the same time. Once the snack is gone, the gum is still in there, probably all mixed up with leftover bits of food. Yuck. And of course we're not even supposed to have gum in school.

- **Pablo:** Quiet, book smart—probably not people smart. Also, it looks like he never cleans his glasses.

- **Erica:** She may be white, but if you close your eyes and listen to her, she sounds just like Jasmine, Ivy, and most of the other girls in school. Also, she has one volume, all the time: loud. Her clothes are as loud as her mouth.

- **Ivy:** Wears pink from head to toe, even her hair beads. Loves glitter. And crunches numbers the way other people crunch potato chips.

- **Jasmine:** Moves like a dancer. Nice to everyone.

That's as far as I got. Then Jasmine came up and asked what I was working on. When I shared the list with her, she pointed out that I included opinions, but true observing is looking without adding your own thoughts and assumptions. She's right. But it's hard to keep personal opinion out of it.

My final observation for the day: Lists are fun!

1. You can say a lot in a few words.

2. They help organize your thoughts.

3. They're a quick read.

4. They help you remember things.

5. They can be as long or short as you want them to be.

Logging On

Jas and I went to the computer lab after school today. Our plan was to log in to the Science Squad website and see if there were any clues about the four stickers and how to get started earning them.

The room was a jumble of chairs and desks. Ivy sat at one of the computers, doing homework. She was probably typing up that annoying essay assignment Ms. Michaelson gave us today in English class: an essay on the book *Bud, Not Buddy*.

I hate writing essays. Since we don't have a computer at home, I have to write it all out and then take it into the library to type it, or I have to stay after class to use one of the school computers. I wish Ms. Michaelson would let me do a poster instead so that I could draw part of it. Or better yet, say what I have to say in comic book form. I'm going to ask her about it tomorrow.

I almost didn't notice, but Pablo was there too, over in the corner. That kid is *always* studying. I'll bet he studies for fun.

Ivy came over to see what we were up to. If she was a moth, computers would be her flame. The three of us explored the Science Squad site. It turns out the Squad is a lot bigger than our school or even the city. There are chapters all over the country! I didn't realize I'd be a part of something so big. We also found out that some of the Squads work on different projects, like sea turtles in North Carolina, monarch butterflies in Texas, and zombie bees in California.

"Sea turtles?" I said, "Why couldn't we study turtles? Sea turtles rock."

"There's just one problem," Jasmine said. "Sea turtles don't live in New York City."

I had a flash of wishing I lived somewhere else. But I do love the city. With so many people, it's easy to find whatever you're interested in. Art, food from every country you can imagine, the latest in music, fashion, whatever! If I lived in some little town in another state, I might not be able to get my hands on the latest issues of *The Tick* or *The Avengers*.

We didn't find much about the stickers, except that each local chapter handles them differently, depending on the project. Drat! Then we all took turns logging in to our individual accounts—even Pablo, who at some point magically appeared behind us. That kid has some stealth/invisibility skills I'd never noticed before. It hits me—I've never noticed because he's so good at it. He's like a ninja. I'll have to pay more attention to figure out how he does it. I could put some of those techniques to use, especially when TJ is around.

The upper corner of my profile page had tiny icons for each of the stickers, but clicking on them didn't do anything. Maybe because I haven't earned any yet? I clicked on the "data entry" page. It was completely blank, with no clues about what the project will be. I hope we find out exactly what we'll be doing soon. And I hope it isn't too gross. I sure don't want to have to touch the pigeons and catch some nasty disease. That's where I draw the line.

Ivy figured out how to personalize our avatars and profile pages, so we set them up. I chose a falcon for my avatar. Pablo chose the superhero the Falcon, who is not only an Avenger but can also communicate telepathically with his pet falcon, making me wish *I* had thought to pick him.

As we were finishing up, a couple of eighth graders swaggered in. They looked us over. "You're The Mouth's little bro, right?"

I nodded, and they gave me fist bumps like I was one of them. Out of the corner of my eye, I could see Pablo and Ivy taking it in, mouths agape. Thank you, Mouth! I only wish the other guys in the Squad could have seen.

I left school feeling pumped, like somehow, my world got a little wider today.

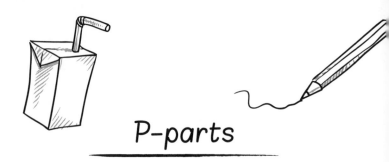

P-parts

It's two in the morning and I'm STILL awake. Not for a good reason, like because I'm sneaking a couple rounds of video games—no, it's because my legs hurt so much they are keeping me awake. The pain is dull, but it won't let up. Maybe it's the Blount's disease acting up again. I'm worried the leg braces aren't enough to keep it in check anymore. Maybe I should wake Mom. But she has to work early, and I don't want her to blow this out of proportion.

The Mouth is snoring. I'm not going to wake him either because when it comes to my legs, he'd take it straight to Mom. No, I'm on my own. Since I'm probably going to be up all night, I need to distract myself. I click on my bedside light and pull out my notebook. I guess I'll study the pigeon parts Miss Diesha asked us to learn by the next meeting.

I cannot get these pigeon parts to stick in my head. Here's an observation: It's easier to learn about something when you're interested in it. The less you're into something, the harder it is for the information to stick. For example, the people who really like pigeons, like Jasmine and Neeko, will probably learn these parts in half the time it will take me. On the other hand, I know every Marvel comic character and their powers, and I can name just about every dinosaur there is.

I tell myself that all this studying will be worth it when I win the overnight trip to the museum. And, once I learn these parts, I'll reward myself by reading comics. There are a couple of issues of *The Tick* that I never get tired of.

Science Squad Meeting #2

We had another Science Squad meeting today. I had to talk to Ms. Michaelson about my essay after school (she said yes to adding drawings, but no to an outright cartoon), so I didn't get there early. The seat next to Jasmine was taken, so I got stuck in the back. And guess who was there? TJ! Ugh. It turns out he's on the Squad after all. He smiled at me in a way that made me feel like a blender had switched on inside my gut. I sat as far away as I could, but his eyes still drilled into the side of my head.

Miss Diesha came into the room, hefting a great big cardboard box. I was afraid it was full of pigeons she was going to release right there and then. But it was only a box of T-shirts—emerald green (a color I love) with the Science Squad motto ("Ask questions, seek answers") on the front, and the Science Squad logo on the back. I'm glad the T-shirts don't have a picture of a beady-eyed you-know-what on them!

Miss Diesha said it's a good idea to wear the shirts when we're working on Project Pigeon Power. That way other people in the community will know we're doing citizen science. Maybe they'll ask questions and get involved too.

Then we got down to business. Miss Diesha asked what we'd noticed since the last meeting. Everyone suddenly got interested in looking at the floor. Even Erica. Actually, she looked like she was trying to stealth text, with a sweater half slung over her phone. The silence became painful, and since I didn't want to disappoint Miss Diesha, I raised my hand. My heart beat real fast, knowing TJ was right there, ready to pounce, but I went ahead and told her about the different colors of pigeons I had seen, and the even fancier ones in the book from Mr. Geo.

Miss Diesha clapped her hands together. "Great work, Anthony! You are very observant. And you just earned an observation sticker! Nicely done."

I felt like a hot ember glowing bright.

Of course TJ added, just low enough so Miss Diesha wouldn't notice, "I'm really observant too. I just observed someone suck up to get a sticker."

Even though I expected it, it felt like a splash of cold water. My glow went out. I sank low in my chair. But the sticker—I had one now, and he didn't.

Then Miss Diesha asked us to name some other kinds of birds, and this time, hands flew up. Jasmine started listing flamingos and puffins and other birds from her T-shirt, but Miss Diesha interrupted to say she meant birds that we see in the city. So Jasmine changed her answer to robins, crows, and sparrows. Erica added seagulls to the list, and then Pablo said falcons.

Miss Diesha said that was a great list and asked us to think about the color patterns of these birds. It didn't take long for us to figure out that even though males and females are sometimes different from each other, each type of bird has its own very predictable color pattern. You don't ever see a crow with red feathers or a robin that's all black.

Ivy slowly raised her hand, like she was trying to figure something out on its way up. "But the pigeons here in NYC are all different colors."

"Bingo!" shouted Miss Diesha. She was so loud everyone jumped. "In fact," she said with excitement, "they're the only kind of wild bird that comes in a whole bunch of different colors. And the big question is, why?"

Apparently, wild pigeons used to all be one color pattern too: gray, with wide black-blue stripes across their wings. Then people started to keep pigeons. They bred them to get different color patterns of blue, red, gray, white, and brown mixed in different ways. Some people also bred them to look like the fancy pigeons in my book.

Some of these pigeons escaped back into the wild. But instead of slowly going back to being the one color pattern they used to be (which Miss Diesha said is what scientists would expect to happen), all the different pigeon color patterns are *still* around.

So here's our Squad's mission: to help scientists like Miss Diesha solve why wild pigeons still come in so many different colors.

And here's how we're going to do it: by counting the different color patterns (which are called color morphs) we see. There are twenty-eight different color morphs, but we're going to use only seven to make counting *easier—if we see something that doesn't fit into these seven patterns, we'll count it as "other."*

Miss Diesha explained that we'd have a quiz on these color morphs at the next meeting. She'll bring in real pigeons, and we'll have to name the body parts and the color morphs.

After we can pick out the different color morphs, we'll go to our pigeon-watching spots to count the number of times we see each color morph.

Then we'll enter our data into a big database and look for clues to figure out what it means. No touching, just looking. YES! I've GOT this!

Then Miss Diesha opened it up to other questions we're curious about. She said questions are an important driving force behind science, so anyone who asked a question backed up by evidence of good thinking and observing would earn an observation sticker.

Everyone's hand shot up. Except mine—I already had my sticker.

Jasmine: "I noticed that sometimes pigeons look like they're dancing together. They follow each other around, bobbing their heads in time. Why do they do that?"

Miss Diesha: "That's part of their courting behavior. Everyone knows what courting means, right? It's when the male tries to impress the female to win her as his mate. Birds' courting behavior can vary greatly, depending on their species. Birds use dances, songs, and nest building to court each other."

Ivy: "Do pigeons pick their mates by color?"

Miss Diesha (beaming): "Great question, especially because this is one of the things scientists want to figure out. In addition to counting different color patterns, we're going to record the colors of courting pigeons. If pigeons do choose mates based on color morph, it might explain why so many different colored pigeons still exist here in the city."

Pablo: "Do pigeons that live in the same area tend to be mostly the same colors?"

Miss Diesha: "Another great question. And one that we might be able to answer from the data you collect. Can anyone think of what might cause that to happen?"

TJ called from the back of the room: "Who cares? We're gonna see some pigeon action." (bobbing his head like a bird) "Come to Papa!"

Lately, I've been noticing just how many goofy comments that kid makes. I used to think he did it to get attention. But now I'm starting to think it's because he doesn't know the answer and wants to cover that up. I think that deep down, he cares that he doesn't know. Neeko will make a joke if he gets a bad grade on a paper or test, but TJ *never* tells anyone what kind of grades he gets.

Miss Diesha's hands flew to her hips. I could tell she was annoyed by TJ, but she ignored him, saying, "Okay, everyone who just asked a question: I'm going to post an observation sticker to your profile page. Being curious and observant are essential qualities if you want to be a great scientist. And keep in mind, this first sticker may be easy, but don't be fooled—you'll have to work harder for the others."

Then she explained that anyone who could name the body parts and the color morphs of the real pigeons she brings in for the quiz will earn a knowledge sticker.

Memorizing all those colors and body parts seems like a lot of work! Still, it feels good to be the first person to earn an observation sticker. This is what my sticker looks like:

Science Squad homework:

- Make flash cards of the seven main pigeon color morphs.
- Memorize the names of the different color morphs.
- Keep studying pigeon parts for the quiz at the next meeting.

Makes Me Wanna . . .

A funny thing happened before science class today while we were waiting on Mr. Mitts. And yes, it had to do with the P-word. Everyone was talking about where they went to do their pigeon watching and how many birds they saw over the weekend. Me, I sunk back into invisibility and worked on some dinosaur sketches, but I kept an ear out.

I heard Neeko say he saw Pablo at a park with his mom. Pablo shrugged. "I'm an only child and my parents are super protective. So what?" Wow. Brave move. If that were me, I would NOT be announcing it to the class. And once again, I'm very glad The Mouth is around to help me with things so it doesn't always have to be Mom.

Neeko laughed and asked Pablo if his parents still tie his shoes for him.

Pablo said, "Nah, I wear Velcro," even though he doesn't. This made Neeko look down. TJ burst out, "Made you look, made you stare, now give us your underwear!" Neeko and TJ started pushing and grabbing at each other while Pablo sunk back into the shadows like a ninja.

Erica's voice soared above everyone else's. She said she saw so many pigeons, she knows she's going to be the Squad's top member. But when everyone asked her where, she wouldn't tell. Ha. Maybe she's just making it up. She'll do anything for attention.

I'm the opposite. I find it works best when other people (like TJ) don't notice you. No attention means no bad attention, and from my experience, most of the attention that I get at school is bad. That's why my strategy in class (or on the playground) is to blend into the background as much as possible. Hood up, eyes down, speak only when necessary. Things aren't perfect, but it would be much worse if I made myself more noticeable.

Neeko said his dad has a friend who keeps pigeons in Brooklyn, so he's just going to use those. Maybe that's why he's so into pigeons. Anyway, that started an argument between Ivy and Neeko about whether the Science Squad cares if the pigeons we watch are wild.

Also, Brooklyn isn't all that close, so it might not work for him anyway.

I was just thinking, *If I have to hear another word about pigeons, I think I'll . . .* when Neeko called out, "I'm so done talking about this. Watching pigeons makes me want to sit on the TV and watch the couch!"

A loud laugh exploded out of me. I clapped my hand over my mouth. Other kids laughed too. He probably got it from online—people sometimes go crazy with "Makes me want to" comments on hip-hop videos. Soon everyone was snapping words back and forth, trying to one-up each other. The lines were so good, I wrote them down:

Erica: "Watching pigeons makes me wanna eat my spoon with my cereal."

Jasmine: "Watching pigeons makes me wanna do my homework and never turn it in." (Yeah, right, that'll be the day!)

Neeko again: "Yeah, it makes me wanna study after the exam." (Well, he doesn't study before exams either.)

Pablo: "Watching pigeons makes me wanna listen to my music on mute!"

I wanted to join in, but as hard as I thought, I couldn't come up with one. So I kept pretending I was drawing. Once again, I had the feeling of being on the outside, invisible, partly by choice, but partly not. That make me think of one: "Watching pigeons makes me want to draw my comics in invisible ink." Not bad, if I do say so myself!

Ivy: "Watching pigeons makes me wanna divide by zero." (I swear that girl is obsessed with numbers!)

Everyone was laughing when TJ came in a few beats late: "Watching pigeons makes me wanna wipe my butt before I go. No, even better—makes me want to strut my stuff like Anthony!"

I think it got quiet after that, but I don't know if it was because of TJ's comment or because Mr. Mitts walked in at that very moment.

"Mr. Mitts!" called Neeko. "Taking Mr. Mitts's science class makes me want to take a shower without water!"

And everyone was off again. But that didn't change the fact that I hate TJ.

Bored in Gym Class

Sometimes I wish gym class didn't exist. Because of the problems with my legs, I can't play sports like the rest of the kids. I have a note from my doctor explaining why, but it's boring to just sit and watch. This week, Jasmine got permission to sit out because she hurt her ankle in dance class. But she spent the whole time talking to a couple other girls who were also sitting out. Even though Jasmine is a great friend, it's not like I want to do everything with her, or even all the same things as her. Plus, I'm not really all that interested in hanging out with the other girls, and I'm pretty sure it's mutual. So, I ended up just waiting for the time to pass.

Today I was so bored that I actually looked around to see if there were any pigeons in sight.

There weren't.

With nothing else to do, I sat down and drew a quick Dino Tech Destroyers comic:

I was just finishing up when I heard shouting. The basketball game had turned pretty serious. It was so action packed, I got pulled into watching. Even Pablo got into it. And TJ is actually really good. He's big and fast and has a great layup. I'd be impressed if he wasn't such a jerk.

One of these days when I don't have to wear braces anymore, I'm going to run laps all over the city.

Flash Card Factory

After school, I went over to Jasmine's to work on the pigeon flash cards. I made one flash card for each feather pattern we need to know for the quiz:

- **Blue-bar:** A pigeon with a dark gray body, two black stripes (called bars) on each wing, and shiny, rainbow-like neck feathers.
- **Spread:** A pigeon that is all black or dark gray.
- **Red-bar:** A pigeon with a brown or rusty-red body and light gray wings with two reddish brown bars on each wing.
- **Red:** Another pigeon with a rusty-red or brown body, but with light gray bars on its wings.
- **Checker:** A pigeon with black and white checks on its wings.
- **Pied:** Any pigeon with splashes of white.
- **White:** Just what it sounds like: a solid white pigeon.
- **Other:** Any pattern that doesn't fit one of the other categories.

Of course Little Lou was there, because she's ALWAYS home (how many places can a three-year-old go?). But it was fun—until Ivy showed up. As soon as she got there, Jas stopped talking to me about music and started talking to Ivy about their dance class.

Ugh.

Lou and Ivy were all over my colored pencils. I don't mind sharing, but they kept sharpening them. The blue, gray, black, and brown ones are getting too short. And since I bought these with my own money, for cartooning, I can tell you they aren't cheap.

I tried to concentrate on making my cards, but I looked up from drawing a white pigeon with red spots on the "Other" card to see Ivy sharpening the gray pencil again. I have to admit, it bothered me way more that she was the one doing it and not Jasmine. When Little Lou put the pink pencil in her mouth, I had had enough. I asked Jas to make sure her little sister didn't ruin my pencils. She snapped back, "Tell her yourself. Besides, you don't even like pink." Then Lou looked at me with her big brown eyes, and even though she was chewing on MY pencil, I felt like a jerk.

Why couldn't it be just me and Jasmine?

Usually when Ivy is around, we don't have much to say to each other. I think it's cool that she's into numbers, but they aren't exactly a conversation starter. She isn't into comics or dinosaurs, and I am definitely NOT into kittens or pink. That doesn't leave much to talk about.

I thought about grabbing my stuff and leaving, but then Ivy started telling funny stories about things that happened at her mom's hair salon. Get this—her mom found a human tooth inside someone's braided hair extensions, and the person had NO idea how it got there or whose it was. How is that possible?

We tried to come up with an explanation, but we were laughing too hard to say anything that made sense. Then Ivy and Jasmine pointed out that Miss Diesha has thick braids too. But she's so put together, we all agreed nothing nasty would ever get into hers.

Ivy had a ton of other stories about the salon, and she's good at telling them. She can make even small things, like getting braids that are too tight or a bad haircut, sound hilarious. I got really into coloring my pigeon cards as I listened, and I forgot all about the pencils.

Suddenly, I realized that I was having fun. It was fun to be working on the same project together, and pretty soon, Jasmine, Ivy, and I each had our own set of pigeon cards.

And Little Lou had a set of snug bugs—scribbled ovals she claimed were bugs wrapped inside blankets. I wouldn't say it out loud, but what a waste of my pencils. Still, Lou pointed to each splotch and told us all about the bug inside each scribble. To make up for earlier, I asked her questions about her bugs. When she wanted to give me one, I took it and acted like it was a great gift that I would cherish forever.

Lou's Scribble Bugs

Science Squad Meeting #3
(A DISASTER)

The Science Squad meeting today couldn't have gone more awfully, terribly wrong!!! I am still very upset and angry about it. But first, the good stuff:

The meeting started off great. I couldn't believe it: Everyone A) noticed my flash cards and B) loved them! Erica told me I was really good at drawing and asked me to make her a set. Even Neeko and Pablo crowded in for a look and called them sweet. Pablo said I should draw comics. Which made me feel great.

And I aced the quiz! I even correctly ID'd the three live birds that Miss Diesha brought in. This time, they stayed inside their crates. Whew.

While I was studying one of them, trying to figure out if it was checkered or pied, its eyes met mine. It gave me a challenging look, like it knew I didn't like it. But I stared it down. And then I figured out it was a pied, which is a tricky pattern because the white splotch could be anywhere on the pigeon, and sometimes you really have to look for it.

Jasmine and Ivy passed the quiz too. We gave each other high fives. Grouping things is actually kind of fun. And after yesterday, I've decided Ivy's really not that bad.

Miss Diesha gave everyone who passed the quiz a pencil topped with a cool brain-shaped eraser. She also told us that a knowledge sticker would show up on our profile page. Two stickers down, two to go. I now know my feathered enemy and am ready for the next challenge.

Miss Diesha said that if you didn't pass this time, not to give up, because there would be another chance at the next meeting. I looked around to see who wasn't holding a brain-eraser pencil. TJ. That was it. No surprise—he hadn't made any ID cards either. He probably didn't even study. Ha. Pretty much everyone else passed—even Neeko, who doesn't care about school. Apparently, brain power is not TJ's strong point.

I could tell TJ was bothered because he went to the back of the class and stayed there kind of quiet with a dark look on his face, like he could bite the head off a pigeon, or whoever else got too close. Well, he deserves to fail if he doesn't work at it.

Miss Diesha told us that the Science Squad was now ready to go out into the real world and work on earning the fieldwork sticker by collecting data.

Finally! This is what we have to do: Go to our pigeon "hangout" and count the number of pigeons of each color morph. At the same time, we'll watch for courting behaviors. Miss Diesha gave us each a handout explaining common behaviors. If we see any, we'll mark down the colors of the two pigeons involved.

Over the next few weeks, we have to go as many times and collect as much data as we can. We'll enter it into a big database on the Science Squad website. Then we'll be able to see the data collected by other citizen scientists just like us. And maybe it will lead to answers.

Ivy wanted to know just how we're going to analyze the data. It figures, since she loves analyzing everything. Miss Diesha said she is setting up a program to help us find patterns in the data, and that she'd tell us more about it soon. But right now, we needed to pick a teammate. She said we'd collect more accurate data if we helped each other and worked in pairs.

I wanted to be with Jasmine, but Ivy cornered her too fast. Jasmine gave me a small shrug. "Sorry," she mouthed. Huh. All my warm feelings about Ivy shriveled up in warp speed. Why couldn't she have paired up with Erica for once?

All around me, kids were finding partners faster than I could think. Within seconds, Pablo and Neeko had paired up. The only other person without a partner was TJ. He was still at the back of the class not paying attention, or he would have joined up with one of the other guys fast.

Miss Diesha must have seen that we were the only two left. "Perfect," she beamed as she packed up her stuff. "Anthony and TJ, you two can work together!"

No WAY! All the blood rushed down to my feet. I felt cold, hot, and dizzy. When I tried to talk, no words came out.

Everyone filed out of the classroom, even Jasmine. Soon it was just me and TJ.

"Okay, Pidge," he said, "I guess we'll be watching your little bird friends together. If I don't stomp their little heads in first." Then he took off too.

Nononononononononononono.

Pigeons AND TJ?

I ran out into the hallway to see if I could catch Miss Diesha. But she was gone.

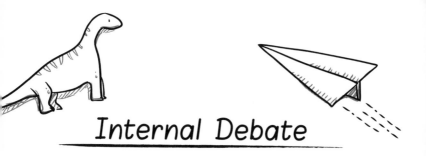

Internal Debate

I'd rather quit Science Squad than partner with TJ. But I don't want him to get the better of me—not again. And I want that fieldwork sticker! I thought about asking Jasmine to come along the first time I meet TJ at the park—TJ doesn't tease her—but she's got a packed schedule, between dance and watching Little Lou. I wanted to ask The Mouth, but then it might look like I'm not allowed to go out alone, even though I am.

So . . . I guess I need to get over it and do it.

Besides, we're going to be counting pigeons. Who says we need to talk? Or even stand near each other?

At least we'll be meeting at my park. When we texted to set up a meeting time and place, TJ actually sounded kind of normal. But maybe that's because texts are so short. He said he hadn't figured out a good pigeon-watching spot (surprise, surprise), so we're going to use mine. This is good because the park is close to home and easy for me to get to, and there are usually lots of people there. That lowers the chance of TJ doing something really mean, and makes it easier for me to escape if I need to.

At the
Park with TJ

TJ and I met at the park after lunch. I almost got in trouble with Mom because I tried to leave without my leg braces. She doesn't get that TJ would tease me about them.

I had my Science Squad T-shirt on, but I felt stupid for wearing it when I saw that TJ hadn't bothered.

TJ: "Hey, can I see your flash cards? I forgot mine."

Me: "I guess."

It was hard handing them over. I'm pretty sure he hadn't bothered to make any. What if he ripped them up? But then again, he was on my team, so what could I do? He flipped through them and made a grunt sound. Disgust or approval? I couldn't tell.

Not a pigeon was in sight, and I was nervous they weren't going to show. I had planned to bring a sandwich and eat it to attract them, but it was back at home, sitting on the kitchen counter. Actually, it was probably in *The Mouth's* stomach by now. Plus, my stomach was in no mood for food. Being at the park with TJ was real awkward, like eating soup with a fork. But at least he wasn't as mean as at school. He didn't say much, just kept picking up my cards and looking at them, which was annoying.

As I looked around for pigeons, I recognized the old guy from my last visit to the park. He was sitting on the same bench as before, reading the same thick book. And he looked as grumpy as ever. Maybe it was because he hadn't left that position in days, and he was hungry and tired and needed to pee.

TJ: "I thought you said there were pigeons here."

Me: "I dunno. They were here last time."

I was ready to head home in humiliation when a woman stopped her stroller by our bench and pulled out crunchy cereal snacks for her toddler. Like magic, pigeons appeared. It's like they pulled off invisibility cloaks or oozed out of the gutters or materialized through a hidden portal. A minute ago, there were none, but now there were plenty. Whew!

Collecting pigeon data might actually work out after all. We started counting. That is to say, *I* started counting. I called out what I saw, and TJ marked it down on our tally sheet, which had a box for each of the seven morphs, plus one box for "Other." At the bottom of the sheet, there was a place to mark the color morphs of courting birds too. It looked like this:

a. Flock Count
Count the size of the flock...

|||| |||| ||||
|||| |||| **24**

b. Color Count
Tally the numbers of each color morph...

Blue-bar	Red-bar	Spread	Red	Pied	Checker	White	Other

b. Courting Count
Circle the color morphs of the courting birds.

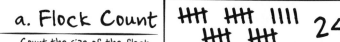

(Blue-bar)	Red-bar	Spread	Red	Pied	Checker	White	Other	(Blue-bar)	Red-bar	Spread	Red	Pied	Checker	White	Other
(Blue-bar)	Red-bar	Spread	Red	Pied	Checker	White	Other	Blue-bar	Red-bar	(Spread)	Red	Pied	Checker	White	Other
Blue-bar	Red-bar	(Spread)	Red	Pied	Checker	White	Other	Blue-bar	Red-bar	Spread	Red	Pied	Checker	White	(Other)
Blue-bar	Red-bar	Spread	Red	Pied	Checker	White	Other	Blue-bar	Red-bar	Spread	Red	Pied	Checker	White	Other
Blue-bar	Red-bar	Spread	Red	Pied	Checker	White	Other	Blue-bar	Red-bar	Spread	Red	Pied	Checker	White	Other

It was tricky, since the pigeons kept moving around. Still, it was going much better than I had thought. Then Neeko showed up. What was he even doing in my park? I've never seen him on this block before. It occurred to me that TJ must have told him we'd be there. Maybe TJ didn't want to be alone with me any more than I wanted to be alone with him.

All of TJ's attention went to Neeko. They horsed around, imitating some music video and pretend fighting each other. They totally ignored me. Which is fine. This feeling grew inside me, like if I had to see Neeko's neon getup and fake jewelry out of the corner of my eyes for much longer, my eyeballs would fry. I got up and left without saying goodbye.

Of course, that's when they noticed me. TJ yelled, "See ya, Pidge," in a loud voice. And the way he said Pidge? It was covered with yuck. I was almost out of the park when he added, loud enough for everyone on the block to hear, "Hey, Pidge, Yo' Mama is so poor, when she goes to the park, the pigeons throw her bread."

I could feel the old guy watching me as I hurried past. I glanced down at the tally sheet and could see that what TJ had marked didn't agree with the types and numbers of pigeons I been calling out. He had marked "White" over and over, even though we hadn't seen any of those. Why, oh why, had I trusted him to record the data for us? Now on top of it all, I was going to have to throw out the day's count. Miss Diesha made it very clear that it's unethical and just plain wrong to fake data. Argh! Of all people, why did I have to be paired with TJ?

I was almost back home when I ran into The Mouth. He must have read my bad mood, because he said, "Hey, little man, looks like you could use some turning around. Come on!" He spun me around by my shoulders and led me to the nearest subway station.

I asked him where we were going, but he just smiled. We got on the green line and headed toward East Village. And so here I am, sitting on the subway, writing this. I figured The Mouth was dragging me along on some errand he had to run for Mom. But he just told me we are getting off at Astor Place. Yes!! Now I know we're headed to the one place I really want to go: St. Mark's.

Crazy for Comics

St. Mark's is a comic lover's delight. It's an old-school, mom-and-pop comic shop, small and cramped with wall-to-wall comics. I LOVE it. When I walked in, the *Star Wars* anthem was playing—this was meant to be. Knowing I'd want to browse for a while, The Mouth said he was going to pop around the corner to get something to eat.

The place has so many treasures tucked into every corner, just waiting to be discovered: every comic you can imagine, plus action figures, lunch boxes, and T-shirts. I scanned the graphic novels first, approaching them with caution since they can have some pretty disturbing stuff inside. Then I headed over to where the Marvel comics were. I scoped out *Moon Girl* and *Devil Dinosaur,* a newer series. Since it features a dinosaur, it's direct competition to my Dino Tech Destroyers idea. Okay, yes, my comic is also going to have super-powered dinosaurs. The key difference is that mine will have <u>lots</u>

of dinosaur characters instead of only one bright-red *T. rex*. And while my human characters are going to be mainly brown like the ones in *Moon Girl*, my story is going to be bigger, better, and have way more fighting. Compared to anything else out there, it'll be EPIC!

As much as I love reading comics, I want to make them even more. When I look at a comic, I think about all the hours the artist put into drawing it.

Actually, I read online that for the bigger comic publishers like DC Comics and Marvel, it takes a whole team to make a comic. There's a writer who comes up with ideas, a penciller who draws out the scenes, an inker, and a colorist. There's even a letterer who writes inside the word balloons and draws the sound effects.

Some of the smaller comics are made by just one guy who does it all. That's how I want to do it. I figure I need to get good at every part if I'm going to have a successful line of comics. The problem is that I have all these ideas, but once I get started on the first couple of pages, my drawings don't look the way I want them to, so I stop.

I was standing in front of a rack of comics, thinking about all this stuff, when I noticed the store clerk watching me. He probably wanted to make sure I wasn't wrinkling up comic book pages. But I know all about how to handle comics—carefully, so that collectors will still want them. Sure enough, after giving me the eagle eye for a bit, the clerk backed off.

By the time The Mouth got back, I had picked out two issues of *The Tick*. The Tick is so funny! He's a giant, blue, insane superhero who just got out of a mental institution. He can't remember anything and has silly superpowers like drama power, reality denial, and nigh-invulnerability. The cartoon and TV shows about him are pretty good, but the original comics are the best. I had just enough money to get the issues I wanted, but since it was back at the apartment in my money jar, The Mouth fronted me the cash. I love that guy!

I read the comics on the ride home. I laughed so hard that The Mouth wanted to read one. He dug in and started laughing too. The Tick is one crazy guy. Which reminds me, there are different kinds of crazy—a funny (even good) kind, and a bad kind that makes you want to run hard in the opposite direction, like the craziness of me being paired with TJ. I need remember to stay sane and keep my eyes on the prize, no matter what TJ pulls.

More Facts That Make Me Like Pigeons Even Less

The more I learn about pigeons, the less I like them:

- They can live just about anywhere.
- They can mate any time of the year, all year long, making more and more pigeons.

Ugh. They really are like cockroaches! I have visions of them multiplying until Earth is covered in pigeons, which inspires me to search for the soundtrack to that old Alfred Hitchcock horror movie, *The Birds*. I haven't seen the whole thing, just scenes where flocks of bird attack people.

Still, I want that fieldwork sticker, so I've been studying the handout Miss Diesha gave us about pigeon courting behavior. Here are some of the things the male will do when he's trying to impress the female:

- **Bowing:** He puffs out his neck feathers, lowers his head, and struts around in a circle.

• **Tail dragging:** He spreads his tail feathers and drags them on the ground.

• **Driving:** He chases after the female, following her closely.

If the girl pigeon likes him, they'll give each other gross pigeon kisses, which scientists call "billing." The male opens his beak, and the female puts her beak inside his. UGH! Pigeons making out? I hope that is something I NEVER have to see!

Once two pigeons choose each other as mates, the female pigeon lays eggs. She lays one to three eggs at a time, two to four times a year. That equals a lot of pigeon babies. It makes me wonder: Why have I never seen a pigeon baby?

Fried Pigeon Backsides

Jasmine came over yesterday after dinner because she needed a break from Little Lou. It wasn't until she took out her set of pigeon flash cards that I realized TJ still had mine! I want them back RIGHT NOW, but I guess I have to wait until next time I see him. No way am I going to call or text him. Not after the lame comments he made at the park.

Jas brought a card game called Exploding Kittens—not that she would ever do *anything* to even come close to hurting a kitten in real life. We put on some upbeat music, broke out a bag of chips and some salsa, and played a few rounds. I really like the art on the cards. And it's not a bad game either—it's a good mix of strategy and chance.

One of the nice things about Jasmine is that unlike a lot of girls I know, she doesn't have to talk all the time, although she does like to talk a lot around certain people, like Ivy. I almost told her that my legs are bothering me again—at night, at least—but I didn't want to ruin the good thing we had going. By the time the bag of chips was gone, we'd won three games apiece and decided to leave it at that.

Playing inspired me to make a game of my own.

Me: "I'll call it Headless Pigeons!"

Jasmine: "Ha! Actually, did you know that pigeons can drop their tail feathers to avoid predators? So they're not headless, just back-end-less."

We looked it up on her phone. She was right. If a predator tries to grab or bite a pigeon from the back, those feathers break away. The predator is left with a mouthful of feathers while the pigeon makes its escape.

So I decided to dump the headless idea and change the game to "Fried Pigeon Backsides." First you have to scare the pigeons. Then you collect as many backsides as you can. We spent the rest of our time brainstorming lists of rules for how to play.

Nighttime Worries

My legs hurt and I can't sleep.

Sometimes at night, all my worries float to the surface of my brain, like plastic toys in a tub of water. Things like:

- What's happening with my legs? Why do they hurt like this?
- What if I always have to wear leg braces?
- Will I ever have a crew of friends like The Mouth does?
- Why is Jasmine even friends with me? Everyone likes her. She's nice and popular and can walk normally. Is it just because we live in the same building? If we lived across town from each other, would she even bother?

I'll probably always walk funny. Maybe I'll be a grown-up and everyone will STILL call me Pidge. If that happens, I'm going to move far, far away* where no one knows me and never come back.

*It will definitely be a place with NO pigeons!

The Kick

Stupid TJ was supposed to meet me at the park today but never showed up. Well, I'm going to get that fieldwork sticker even if he isn't going to try. And no way is he keeping my flash cards.

The old guy was there again. He must live in the park! But how does he manage to be so well dressed? Also, he doesn't smell the way homeless people sometimes do. I hope he has somewhere to go when it gets dark or rains. And if he can read a big book like that, he must be pretty smart. I wonder what it's about—one of these days I'll get close enough and use my powers of observation to find out.

Today, the birds crowded around the old guy's feet even though he wasn't eating. They must have been annoying him, because right before my eyes, he kicked at one of them! Imagine a battering ram as big as your body flying at you, top speed. That's what it must have been like for the pigeon. The little guy managed to duck out of the way—mostly—but the guy's foot definitely made some contact. That's when I noticed the pigeon had a funny walk. Like something was wrong with its leg or foot.

I may hate pigeons, but I still don't want to see them get hurt. So without thinking it out, I marched over to the grumpy guy's bench.

Me: "Hi. You don't know me, but I see you here all the time, and um, I just saw you kick at that pigeon. Please don't do that. I can't stand pigeons either, but the more I get to know about them, the more I realize they're not all bad." Then I told him about Mon Cheri and the rescue birds that used to be trained to spot people who were lost in the ocean from helicopters. (I read that in the book from Mr. Geo.)

The grumpy guy just glared at me, silent, so I figured maybe he thought I was making the whole thing up. So I kept talking. I told him about the Science Squad, and how I needed to count color morphs, and how I was trying to be more observant, and would he please just leave the pigeons alone so I could do what I needed to do?

I waited for an explosion, but instead he smiled and tipped his hat. "Okay," he said. The he turned back to his book.

Okay? Did that mean no more kicking? Was it that easy? I lingered for a moment, not sure what else to say. Realizing this was my chance to find out what he was reading, I inched closer. The title was *Cognitive Psychology:* something something something. I couldn't understand what it meant. But it confirmed that he was no dummy. He didn't look up again, so I wandered away.

Back at my own bench, I pulled out the peanut butter sandwich I remembered to bring this time. When the pigeons caught sight of this, they came to me and left the old guy alone. I spotted the one with the hurt leg—a gray pigeon with splashes of white, including a white blotch on the top its head. Its foot was mashed up, and it looked like a long-term injury, not something caused by the old guy's kick. I tossed a bit of bread in the bird's direction. He ate it in two pecks. Then we eyed each other. It wasn't like the time Miss Diesha's pigeon and I had a stare-down. This was different. Like we were communicating.

After that, I couldn't keep my eyes off him. He had more trouble walking than the other birds, but he did pretty well. I got into watching how the birds interacted with him and with each other. He was more timid than some of the others, darting away when any of them got too close. Maybe it was because he'd just been kicked. But then his curiosity would win out, and he'd circle back to join the outer edges of the flock. I could relate.

Scrapper. That's what I'm naming him.

Another pigeon darted in and around all the others, like an insane windup toy. He must have eaten a pile of coffee grounds for breakfast. And a third strutted around slow with his neck feathers puffed to the max, like he was king and all the other pigeons should stop and pay their respects. Which they didn't. I never would have believed it if I didn't see it with my own eyes—these little guys have personality, just like people!

As I watched, I collected some data. I was feeling pretty good, until I got up to walk home. Sharp pains shot up my legs. My braces felt like they were squeezing my legs way too tight. Each step was harder and harder to take. I've never been so relieved to see the entrance of my building. Then I had another stab of discomfort: If this kept happening, I'd have no choice but to tell Mom.

Scrapper

My legs feel much better today. Even though it's longer, Jasmine and I took a different route home from school so we could pass by the park. Jas and Ivy have been going to the square near their dance studio to count pigeons before and after class. But after hearing my pigeon-kicking story, Jasmine wanted to see what Mr. Grump looked like. I knew she was secretly hoping to see him take a swipe at another pigeon so she could give him a piece of her mind. Jasmine is not one to stand by when an animal is being treated unfairly. Take the spiders in my room—she's singlehandedly saved most of them from being smushed.

For once, the old guy wasn't there. That didn't stop Jasmine and me from brainstorming facts we could use to convince him he shouldn't be mean to pigeons. Here's our list:

- Pigeons can remember who is nice and who is mean to them.

- People brought the first pigeons to New York, so technically, it's not the pigeons' fault they're here.
- Pigeons are very adaptable, so they have gotten used to people and don't mind lots of noise.

Note: This list does NOT mean I've started liking pigeons. I haven't. Except for maybe Scrapper.

Speaking of which, I was able to show Scrapper to Jasmine. He stands out not just because of his walk, but also because of his unique markings. Especially the white spot on the top of his head. When I pulled out a bag holding some sandwich crusts, he came right over to me. A few crumbs landed on my shoe by accident, and he pecked them off! That gave me the idea of training him to eat out of my hand. But when I lowered a crumb-filled hand down to his level, all the other pigeons appeared, crowding in to look for food, and Scrapper was pushed to the outer edges.

Jasmine said he was handsome (of course she thinks so—she would think a sea slug was handsome!) and then got up to go. I got up too. I wanted to get home for dinner before The Mouth ate everything on the table.

In My Face

I am NOT going to work with TJ anymore! The next time we have a meeting, I need to tell Miss Diesha. I don't even care if it gets me kicked off the Squad.

TJ was supposed to meet me to collect pigeon data, but he was late. Mr. Grump was there again though. He nodded at me and went back to reading. When Scrapper showed up, I slipped him some crumbs from the bag inside my pocket. I swear he now makes a beeline for me, even though the park is full of people. And I haven't seen him anywhere near Mr. Grump's bench since the kick. Pretty smart.

Then I got down to it. I saw ten pieds, fifteen blue-bars, three reds, and four checkers. I'm starting to pick up on courting behaviors too. I watched a male checker follow a female blue-bar around, first dragging his tail feathers and then chasing her. The way their heads bobbed to the same imaginary beat reminded me of a synchronized dance.

TJ finally showed just as I was finishing. He didn't say anything about being late. No "Sorry to keep you waiting," or "I missed my train." He just asked how much data I'd gotten and if he could see it. That got to me. I am not going to do all the work and have him take credit too.

I told him we should count some more color morphs, that he could count and I'd mark them down this time. But he refused. He grabbed the clipboard from me and said he'd mark stuff down. Yeah, right. When I insisted we take turns (partly because I wanted to make sure we collected *real* data, not just stuff he made up), he just sat there, looking at the pigeons like a dope. There were three pied pigeons right there under his nose, and he didn't name them for me to tally. Then a red-bar showed up. Still nothing. I was getting more and more irritated. And my legs were achy, which always shortens my fuse.

Then he had the nerve to ask how much data we needed to earn a fieldwork sticker. I was fed up. At that moment, I noticed the top edges of my flash cards sticking out of his back pocket. That's right—he'd been keeping them in his back pocket! They were probably all dirty and bent at this point, or worse yet, molded to his butt.

Me: "No way are you going to take credit for any data I collected on my own. And give me my flash cards back! NOW!"

TJ: "Flash cards? I don't have any flash cards."

ARGH! My head filled with the buzz of angry wasps. Did he think I was stupid or something? I wanted to scream "Liar!" in his face. But I knew he could beat me into a pulp if he wanted, so I didn't. I just said real quiet, "You're lying. I can see them in your pocket, and you'd better give them back to me right now. Just because you're slacking at Science Squad doesn't mean you get to take my stuff."

He sprang up from the bench we were sitting on, and for a second, I thought he was going to take a swing at me. I felt dizzy. But instead, he whipped the cards out from his pocket and threw them in my face.

"Take your stupid cards. They suck, you suck, and this pigeon project sucks! Little Pidgey-widgy."

Then he imitated the way I walk, bobbing his head way harder than any self-respecting pigeon, and stormed off.

I stood there stunned. That was a very visible scene, in a very public place. When I got the nerve to look around, a young couple and of course the old guy were watching me. Even Scrapper, who had moved off to the grass, seemed to be watching. Heat rose into my cheeks, like they were slathered in hot sauce. I got off the bench and picked up the cards, one by one. One of them had landed in a blop of ketchup, one had grains of yellow rice stuck to it (right on the pigeon drawing's beak, which would have been funny under other circumstances),

and two of the others were smudged with dirt. And yes, they were all curved to fit his butt.

I tried to forget about it and collect some more pigeon data, but I couldn't focus. TJ's angry face kept appearing in front of me. His expression right before he threw the cards reminded me of myself when people want to talk about my legs. It makes me angry-scared, like I wanted to yell to push it all away, except I never can. What is that kid's deal, anyway? Why did he even join the Squad if he doesn't care about it?

Mr. Grump surprised me by getting up and walking over to me. He introduced himself as Mr. Garamelli. (Italian—I knew it!) "That kid ain't nice. Not like you," he said. "And you're right I shouldn't be kicking at pigeons. They may be annoying, but that doesn't mean they deserve a boot to the head." With that, he tipped his hat and kept going, right on out of the park. I wonder where to—a bar, a sandwich shop, to meet with other mob members? Or maybe he's on his way to a big family gathering, with lots of grandchildren? Wherever it is, I hope it's someplace nice.

A Dream

They are after me, even in my dreams.

When I went to bed last night, I left the window open because it gets so dang hot in my room. I could hear The Mouth and his friends talking down on the street, which was comforting. There's a big hole in the window screen, and before I drifted to sleep, I remember wondering if any bugs would come in.

In my dream, a menacing feeling came over me. A hard rock song—one of those fast, driving, angry-sounding ones—was playing. Then a whole flock of pigeons poured into my room, ripping the screen hole even bigger and pecking me all over, right through the covers. It really hurt! Sharp pains stabbed at my legs, and then somehow I knew they were going to go for my head. I could hear TJ's voice calling up from the street, "Get him, boys! Rip him into little bits!"

I woke up in a cold sweat, my legs burning.

I've noticed my legs bother me way more at night than they do during the day. It's hard to know how serious the problem is when the pain fades in and out like that. At night, I lie there, thinking I should go tell Mom. But when day rolls around, it seems silly to bother her about it. Maybe if I pay close attention, I'll be able to figure out exactly what is going on.

Being observant is like hearing music on really good speakers in stereo after listening to it through little tiny speakers plugged into an MP3 player. You really can learn about things—and people—just by keeping your eyes and ears open.

For example:

1. Jasmine talks differently, more sing-songy, when she is with Ivy than when she is talking to me. Which is more real? I like to think it's when she's with me, but I'm going to keep observing to figure that out.

2. When Little Lou watches you eat a cookie that she wants, she'll take an air bite while you sink your teeth into the real thing. I don't think she even knows she's doing it. She just wants it so bad.

3. Pulling the hood of my sweatshirt up over my head is almost like putting on an invisibility cloak.

4. Pablo reads comics on the sly. He keeps one inside his school notebook, just like me. I wonder if he draws too. I'm planning to talk to him about that. Funny how you can see someone in class every day, but you still don't really know them. What you THINK you know isn't always the whole story.

5. TJ hasn't been turning in his homework. Sure, he's known to sometimes forget to bring an assignment in, but this seems different. Like he's falling behind in every class.

Man, all this observing takes a lot of energy. If your head fills up with the endless stream of little stuff, it can make you forget the big stuff. And sometimes the big things (clothes, for example) are important. Yesterday I was so busy noticing the way The Mouth cleaned dirt off his Nikes with an old toothbrush that I almost forgot to put my own sneakers on before heading out the door. Ha! It made me think of TJ and how he forgets things. Now that I've learned to turn my observing powers on, I'll have to make sure to turn them off sometimes too.

Science Squad Meeting #4

Another Friday, another Squad meeting. I got there early with plans to tell Miss Diesha that I couldn't work with TJ. But I didn't have a chance. When she walked in, she immediately called for everyone's attention. She explained that today would be a busy day, and we would be taking turns to enter our data into the Science Squad website. Miss Diesha also pointed out that if we had access to a smartphone, we could download an app to enter data as we collected it, or if we didn't have one (which I don't—mine's an ancient flip phone), we could always enter the data here or at the library each week.

Ivy was so into the idea of entering her data that she was practically panting. When Miss Diesha asked who wanted to type their numbers in first, Ivy jumped into the computer chair. Everyone else, including me, looked at each other and laughed. Ivy joined in too, with a "What? You all know numbers are my thing!"

Neeko elbowed me and said, "Maybe we can get her to enter ALL our data."

Between Neeko acting like I was his bro, and the friendly vibe in the room (which I have NOT felt much in school the past couple of years), I got this squeezy feeling in my chest. Let's just say, it felt right to have the hood of my sweatshirt down for a change.

I've got to hand it to Ivy: That girl can enter numbers like no one else. And she figured out how to access pigeon data from other Squads and scientists, some of who are all the way across the country, or up in Canada, or even across the Atlantic in Europe. But after a bit, Miss Diesha booted her off, saying everyone should take turns to get a feel for the system.

A couple of other kids stepped up next. I could hear them asking Ivy for help. I looked around. TJ wasn't there. Maybe he wouldn't show. I'd have to enter the data myself, but that was fine with me—I was not looking forward to seeing him again.

Pablo had his notebook in hand, with the corner of a *Justice League* comic poking out. I took the plunge and asked him which issue it was. That got us to talking about comics—he' been to St. Mark's too! He's more of a DC comics fan, while I like Marvel, but still. Who knew?

TJ came in and handed a note to Miss Diesha, who nodded at him, so I guess whatever it said made his lateness okay. He ignored me and went right over to Neeko, who had just finished up at the computer. TJ flicked at Neeko's cap and then they fist bumped and joked around. For a second, it reminded me of The Mouth and his crew.

Then it was his and my turn. TJ and me. Talk about awkward. We both stood there looking at the chair in front of the computer. I'd already done so much more than him—no way was I going to do the data entry too, no matter how cool the web page looked. He was shifting around, like he didn't know what to do, or maybe he was just plain unwilling, when a couple of pigeon photos fell out of his notebook. One of them was glued on a piece of a cut-out cereal box to make it stiff. "Blue-bar" was written across the top in messy block letters.

He was making pigeon flash cards!

He picked them up real quick, like he didn't want me to see. But the evidence was there. Maybe he did care about the Squad. Okay, then. Something inside me shifted. I sat down in the chair and said, "You read off the numbers, and I'll type them in."

He was slow about it, but we got through it all, no problem.

Except I could already tell that the amount of data I had (TJ hadn't collected *any* yet.) was not a lot compared to the other groups. They have twice as much data because two kids are doing the work.

Of course, Jasmine and Ivy have the most. Argh! I wish I had been paired with Jasmine—we'd cream everyone else. As it is, TJ and I are way behind. We need a lot more to earn fieldwork stickers.

In fact, TJ still needs to earn the observation and knowledge stickers too. When we checked our profile pages, I was relieved to see the first two stickers lit up next to my name. But there was nothing next to his. When he saw this, he threw up his hands and stalked off, right out of the room. But hey, what did he expect? He hadn't done the work. I seriously do not understand that kid.

Now was my chance to talk to Miss Diesha.

I found her standing in the doorway with her back to me, talking to someone in the hallway who I couldn't see. A man. Their low voices made me curious, so instead of trying to get Miss Diesha's attention right away, I tuned in.

"Family troubles?" she was asking.

"Yes," Now I recognized it was Mr. Mitts's voice. "Between you and me, TJ's parents are divorcing, and he's taking it really hard."

Then he murmured something that I couldn't quite hear: "(murmur murmur) falling behind. The Science Squad is a great way for him to engage at a time when he could use some extra support. So please, work with him, even if he's (more murmuring)."

Miss Diesha: "Thanks for letting me know."

They were talking about TJ! A feeling that I was doing something wrong flooded over me, so I took another step forward.

Me: "Miss Diesha—"

Miss Diesha: "Anthony! I've been meaning to talk to you. I wanted to say that I'm especially glad that you and TJ are on the same team."

I could feel my face twisting up into a scowl. I thought of Mr. Mitts saying TJ needed extra support. What's that supposed to mean? And why should he get extra support if he gives out the opposite? Still, I like Miss Diesha, and once she said she was glad, I didn't feel like I could up and quit being his partner. So I told her he hadn't earned any of the stickers yet, and so far, he hadn't helped with *any* of the data collection. I said I'd keep trying to be his partner but that it felt pretty unfair.

Her brow furrowed.

Miss Diesha: "I'll talk to him."

Me: "Okay. But if he thinks I had anything to do with it, he will KILL me."

Then I took off, quick.

Hmmph. If I want to get that fieldwork sticker, TJ and I are going to have to work together. More than that—we'll have to work double time to catch up with everyone else. But he is:

- Lazy
- Mean
- A bully

And, if I just observe and keep my opinion out of it, he is also:

- Good at sports
- Not so good at school

- *Unhappy*
- *Probably at least a tiny bit interested in pigeons and/or collecting Science Squad stickers to get the Data Collection badge and go on the museum overnight.*

So how can I get him to work with me? For starters, he needs to pass the color morph ID test.

And I think I know how to help him.

Card-Making Factory

Today, instead of working on my cartoons, I made TJ a set of pigeon flash cards. Not for him really, since I think he's a big jerk, but because I want that fieldwork sticker and I'll do what I have to to make sure my team gets enough data. He's got to get up to speed on the different color morphs so he can help me collect data. It would go much faster if we did it together, like we're supposed to.

These cards aren't as detailed as mine, but they still look pretty good. Also, I added arrows to the important parts (like the white spots on a pied or the wing stripes on a blue-bar) to make them easier to pick out. I used up all of my gray colored pencil, so I hope TJ appreciates it. It's a good thing the dinosaurs in my comics are green. At least that's the color I'm making them—with some orange and red. Since no one has ever seen real dino skin, it could be rainbow colored for all we know.

I wonder what TJ will do when I give him these cards?

I can see him throwing them in my face. Then again, I can also see him sliding them into his back pocket.

I also made some pigeon fact cards for Mr. Garamelli—one on pigeons' sense of taste (not very good), one about their breakaway tail feathers, and one on how they're able to read four-letter words. The more he knows about pigeons, the less likely he'll be to kick one. I figure I can add to the set later if he likes them.

Gotta go shake out my hand—it's sore from all that drawing and coloring.

Name: **Doodle Man**

Special Ability: **Able to draw for hours on end with no hand cramps**

Taste Buds

I was in the kitchen earlier this evening when The Mouth came in. He propped open the door to the refrigerator and started pulling out container after container. Soon there was a pile on the counter.

Mom brings home tons of food from the restaurant where she works, which is a good thing, considering how much The Mouth eats. Sometimes she even brings home too much. So at first I thought The Mouth was on a cleaning spree. A lot of that food looked like it should go into a compost bucket. But then The Mouth took out a plate. I watched him put a tortilla on it. Then he opened a container half full of old mac and cheese and dumped it on the tortilla! After that, he added some salsa, a container of hummus, some steamed broccoli, and a scoop of three-bean salad. To top it all off, he squirted on some ketchup.

Ugh! The smell and look of all that food mixed together made my stomach turn. But The Mouth rolled the whole thing up into a massive burrito. He looked at me, grinned, opened his mouth wide . . .

I had to run from the room before I got sick!

I opened the window in my room for some fresh air. Down on the street, I saw some pigeons. They were hanging around an overflowing trash can, pecking at bits of food that had fallen to the ground. This got me thinking . . . The Mouth and pigeons have a lot in common. Like The Mouth, pigeons will eat just about anything. This is probably because pigeons have only forty taste buds and can't taste how gross stuff really is.

I wonder how many taste buds The Mouth has. Most people have about ten thousand, but I'll bet he has less. Sometime when he's asleep, I'm going to look at his tongue—without getting bitten. That guy probably chews on things in his dreams.

More ways The Mouth is a lot like a pigeon:

- Both can find things to eat just about anywhere.
- Both will eat things right off the sidewalk. (Okay, so in The Mouth's case it was in an unopened package, but STILL!)

All this food talk makes me wonder, what DO pigeons eat in the wild?

Another (Bad) Night

Last night was a bad night, and it wasn't just because I was having nightmares about The Mouth eating every gross thing in sight—my legs hurt BAD. I think pain twists up my brain, because in my nightmare, The Mouth turned into one of the *T. rexes* from my comic. He was stomping around, scooping up people, and tossing them into his mouth like crackers. Then he grabbed me. I screamed and yelled for him to stop, that it was me, Anthony, but the next thing I knew, his giant teeth were crushing into my legs.

I must have called out, because I woke up to Mom stroking my forehead. She said she could tell I was in pain by how I was sweating. It was a relief to have her know what I was going through, but now she says I'm going to have to see a doctor. I REALLY don't want to. Mom has already shelled out a lot of cash on account of my legs. She never says anything about it in front of me, but I know it's the reason she's been working extra shifts. Then again, I can't go on for too much longer, with the pain coming and going all the time like this. It's wearing me down.

Mom may overreact about things sometimes, but having her there was like stepping into the air-conditioning on a hot day. What a relief!

P.S. The Mouth slept through it all—another one of his special skills. If he were a superhero, his superpowers would focus on sleep and food. He could fool the fiercest enemy by falling asleep and playing dead, even through serious torture tactics. And then he could eat his way through even the toughest concrete walls and grossest slimy sewage. His battle cry? "Incredible! It's Edible!" just before attacking something with his mouth.

People Morphs

The good thing about my nightmare? It inspired a dinosaur cartoon. In it, the dinos are studying a set of human flash cards, so they can get to know what the people on Earth are all about.

Giving It Out

TJ and I met up after school to do some pigeon watching. When I got there, the park was pretty empty. Of course, Mr. Garamelli was there, reading the same book as always. I'm starting to wonder if he isn't actually a statue or crazy art installation. Like one of those frozen mimes you see in Times Square. If he painted himself all in gold, including his hair and face and everything, he could sit there, just like he already does. Whenever someone gave him money, he'd come to life and turn a page. If they gave him enough, he could get up and bust some moves. Someday I'll spring this idea on him. Maybe he'll pay me a bonus once the money starts rolling in. Today, I just went up to him and handed him the pigeon fact cards.

Me: "Like I said, I don't like pigeons either. But you've got to admit that they can be kind of interesting." (I said this as Scrapper fluttered over. So of course I had to stop and say hello.)

117

Him (I could tell he was trying not to smile): "You don't like pigeons? Funny, I figured you loved them. Isn't your nickname Pidge?

Me: "I hate that name."

Him: "I'll call you something else then. Bird Boy?"

Me: "How about just Anthony?"

Him: "All right then, Anthony." He pointed to my Science Squad T-shirt. " 'Ask questions, seek answers.' I like that. Too many people today think they know everything just because they can look it up on the internet. But the web can't tell you about what's going on right in front of your face, or why the people around you act the way they do."

Me: "Like why you kicked a pigeon?" I clapped my hand over my mouth. Was that rude?

Him (not seeming to care): "Exactly. I was angry about something different entirely, but the pigeon was there, weaker than me, and maybe there was something I didn't like about it—that it can fly and its life is more carefree than mine—so I lashed out at it. It was very wrong of me."

"People do things like that all the time," he continued, tapping the cover of his book, "but that is no excuse. I hope you—and your pigeon friend—will forgive me."

At that moment, TJ slouched into the park, looking miserable. His eyes were red and puffy, like he'd been crying. Was it because of his parents' divorce? And just like that, my brain snapped together what Mr. Garamelli had said with how TJ acts toward me. I've never understood why TJ always picks on me. But maybe it's because he's unhappy about a lot of things that have nothing to do with me. And I do better in school than him, so he lashes out at me.

Or he could just be the school's biggest bully.

I had changed my mind about fifty times about whether to give TJ the new set of flash cards. But when I saw he was wearing his Science Squad T-shirt, that decided it. I went over and handed him the cards.

He didn't say thanks. But he also didn't throw them. After looking at them for a while, he slid them into his jeans pocket. They're his cards, so if he wants them to be butt-formed, that's fine with me.

Mr. Garamelli moved to a bench that was closer to ours, mumbling something about the sun being in his eyes. But really, he just wanted to be able to listen to our conversation. It felt good knowing I had an ally, someone who might step in if TJ suddenly freaked out and got angry on me.

I told TJ I wanted to do some serious data collecting. And he agreed to be the one to tally! Whoa. Miss Diesha must have talked to him. I wonder what she said.

We counted five blue-bars, seven checkers, one spread, and two red-bars. Most of the pigeons came and went, but Scrapper stayed so close that even TJ noticed him.

TJ: "There's no place to mark off 'Bad-leg Pigeon' on the tally sheet."

Me: "I already counted this guy."

TJ: (silence)

Me: "Hey, TJ. Everyone goes through tough times. Including this pigeon. But it makes us stronger, you know?"

TJ (looking at me in surprise and maybe with a little bit of fear): "I guess so." He shrugged. "Gotta go."

Scrapper stayed close as we left the park. And then—I swear I did not imagine this—he started to *follow me home. I'd walk, and he'd flutter around, then land near my feet. I'd keep walking, he'd take off, then flutter back down to land near my feet again. He did this for a whole block! I had to cross a busy street, and I was worried about that, but the crowds of people must have been too much for him, because that's when he took off for good.*

I was happy because: A) he clearly likes me as much as I like him, and B) I didn't want him to get lost or hit by a car. But it was also a little sad to lose his company.

Who would have thought that I, Anthony Briggs, would sort of have a pigeon for a pet?

One Thing That Keeps Me Going

This week, TJ and I met at the park three times. Each time, I was surprised when he showed up. One thing that keeps me going, that motivates me to haul my butt to the park even though each step is a flare of pain, is that I know Scrapper will be there. He flies down to my feet as soon as I sit down on my bench. Once, someone else was already sitting there, so I had to find another bench. I was worried that might confuse Scrapper, but within seconds, there he was. How does he know? Jasmine sure was right about a pigeon's ability to recognize people.

Anyway, we have our pattern. I get there before TJ on purpose. Scrapper comes to greet me, and I feed him. I want him to have a good diet, so I did a little research. I found out that bread is actually bad for pigeons. Instead, they are supposed to eat grains, seeds, greens, berries, and fruits. I felt bad that I'd been feeding Scrapper all those crumbs. So, I found a store that sells a special seed mix designed for pigeons, and I've started feeding him that instead.

Every day, I drop some of the seeds on my sneaker. As he eats them off, I hold my hand, also full of food, close by. One of these days, I'm going to get him to eat right out of my hand.

His pecking around at my feet attracts a bunch of other pigeons that crowd around. With that leg of his, it isn't long before he gets squeezed out of the group. I know how that feels. I wonder, does Scrapper have a group of pigeon friends to hang out with when I'm not here? Are there other people like me, who feed him every day?

What I really want to know is where Scrapper goes when I'm not in the park. He flutters in so quickly, it's hard to tell. Usually he comes from the north end of the park, which is the same direction Mr. Garamelli heads off in on the rare times I've seen him leave the park.

Today, I noticed Mr. Garamelli scattering something at his own feet. I've made him two more cards—one on how pigeons have excellent hearing and can detect really low sounds that humans can't (like the rumble of a distant storm) and another one on something I've noticed on my own: Pigeons do not roost in trees like other birds. They'll perch on building ledges and the tops of lampposts and monkey bar platforms, probably because they are like the rocky cliffs pigeons live on in the wild. But I've never seen one in a tree.

Actually, I've been looking through the book that Mr. Geo gave me and have been brainstorming other interesting ideas for fact cards. Like:

- Pigeons are the only bird that can suck water up through their beaks like a straw. Who knew? Most other birds use their beaks to scoop water and then throw their heads back to swallow.

- Pigeons can keep themselves warm or cool by adjusting how much air they trap with their feathers. That's why pigeons look bigger when it's cold out. They push out their feathers and turn them into insulation. On hot days, they press their feathers down flat to stay cool.

These cards are pretty good. Maybe instead of my "Fried Pigeon Backsides" game, I should design a pigeon trivia game—"Pigeon Pursuit"—with a lot of fact cards.

More Pigeon Watching

TJ and I keep meeting up at the park after school to count pigeons. So far, blue-bars seem to be the most common. But I've been learning that pigeons are creatures of habit, so we might just be counting some of the same birds over and over again.

While I've been bird-watching this week, I've also been TJ-watching. Here's what I've observed:

- His breath smells like peanut butter.
- His handwriting is bad, and he writes very slowly.
- He's been wearing the Science Squad T-shirt a lot.
- He'll put earbuds in and then pretend he can't hear anything you're saying. Argh! So annoying!
- When he plays basketball at recess, it's like he knows where the ball is going to be before it gets there.

I've decided TJ is a little bit like the Tick. Not the brightest, but if he turned his powers to good, he'd be a force to contend with.

Science Squad
Meeting #5

At the meeting today, we all took some time to enter our latest round of data into the Science Squad website. When it was my and TJ's turn, I noticed that TJ now had observation and knowledge stickers next to his name.

"Whoa, when did that happen?" I asked, pointing.

TJ shrugged. "I met with Miss Diesha last week." Then he shouted over to Neeko to keep me from asking anything else.

Ivy asked how much data we needed to have to earn the fieldwork sticker. I was wondering the same thing. TJ and I were doing better than before, but we were still behind everyone else. Miss Diesha glanced at me before answering. "I'm not going to give you an exact number of data points. Some people are collecting in spots where there are fewer pigeons to count, but their work is just as important as the people who collect at busier places."

Ivy sighed.

Miss Diesha continued, "So even though I know you want an exact number, I'm going to ask you to just keep collecting as much as you can for the next couple of weeks. And, start thinking about the final sticker you need to earn for this project: the engagement sticker. You'll want to take everything you know about pigeons, choose a topic to study in greater depth, and share what you've learned with others. This is your chance to get creative and take what you've been learning one step beyond. I want to be wowed!"

Erica called out, "Let's meet at the library later today to figure out what to do to earn those stickers."

Erica, Jasmine, and Ivy all said they'd be there. I heard Neeko agreeing to go too. I wonder if Pablo will go. Heck, I wonder if I will go.

Mr. Mitts stopped in to see how we were doing, just as Miss Diesha was asking us to think about some of the reasons why pigeons are so many colors.

Mr. Mitts jumped in, "Wonderful! We've being learning about hypotheses in science class." (A hypothesis is when you assume an idea is true. Then you test it out with experiments and research.) "Everyone, I want you to come up with a hypothesis to answer Miss Diesha's question. Why do pigeons come in so many colors?"

Miss Diesha: "Yes, who's got one?"

I raised my hand, just in case she suddenly decided to award an engagement sticker to the person with the best hypothesis (spoiler alert: this did *not* happen!). But Miss Diesha called on Erica first.

Erica: "I believe that pigeons keep having different color morphs because this is NYC, a place where fashion matters. These little birds want to stand out from the crowd." (The girls all giggled.)

Neeko: "I think it's just like skin color, and that diversity is a good thing."

Miss Diesha: "Not exactly a hypothesis, but you could certainly shape some of those ideas into one."

My mind raced. I thought of Darwin, his theory of evolution, and how the fittest members of a species— that is, the ones who are best at competing for things they need (like food) and reproducing—are the ones who survive. And how this shapes the species' appearance and behavior over time. Then I thought of Scrapper. An *idea took shape in my head. I wanted to share, but I didn't want to make myself a target. I hesitated, then decided to go for it.*

Me: "My hypothesis is that some colors might be weaker or more likely to have things wrong with them than others colors, but here in the city, there is so much food and room that even weaker birds can survive. There's enough for all the colors."

Pablo added: "They also don't have many natural predators in cities."

Mr. Mitts: "Excellent! That is a solid, testable hypothesis."

Miss Diesha smiled and nodded her head like she was going to shake it off her neck, braids flying: "When food is in short supply, animals will fight among themselves to get it. Only the strongest birds can survive and breed. But here in the city, like Anthony said, there's enough to go around. And Pablo has an excellent point too. Predators tend to pick off the weakest animals in a population. If some colors of pigeons are weaker than others, there aren't a lot of predators here to attack them."

(Gotta play some evil music to write this next line.)

TJ: "Same thing in schools, which explains why Pidge here is still around."

Everyone got quiet and looked around. My face went hot, and I pulled my hood up. I knew I shouldn't have said anything. Any time I talk, TJ goes in for the kill and tries to take me down.

He's the predator, and I'm his prey.

Mr. Mitts told TJ to come with him. After they left the room, some other kids threw out more hypotheses, but I didn't hear any of them. I was hot all over, like I was going to burst into flames. I'm so weak, I did nothing to fight off my predator. Even a pigeon would have tried harder than me.

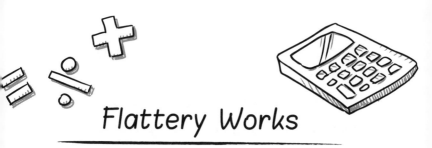

Flattery Works

During math class, Erica and Ivy came and stood by my desk. I didn't look up, I could just kind of feel them there and see Erica's loud flower pattern out of the corner of my eye. I did not want trouble. I reached back for my hood. But before I'd completed the maneuver, Erica said, "Hey, Pidge?"

I considered holding out until she said *Anthony*, but my curiosity got the better of me. Besides, she's probably forgotten my real name by now.

Me: "Yeah?"

Erica: "We're making posters for the sixth grade neighborhood fundraiser, and we were wondering if you would draw some pictures for us."

No way did I want to be the laughingstock again. I could see TJ scribbling all over my posters, bathroom wall graffiti style.

Me: "Thanks, but no thanks."

Erica: "Come on! We liked your color morph flash cards."

Ivy: "Yeah, and the drawings on your binder." (It's covered with Dino Tech Destroyers prototype drawings.)

Erica: "We need you. Nobody else can draw like you."

That got my attention. I looked from one face to another. They weren't kidding.

Flattery works!

Me: "Well . . . okay. Why not?"

If I want everyone to read my comics one day, I have to get used to people looking at my art.

Going Crazy at the Library

Jasmine asked me to come with her to the library to meet everyone. When I said I didn't think I'd been invited, she pulled my arm and said, "Everyone was invited." Sure enough, the only person from the Squad who didn't come was TJ.

"Okay," said Erica, taking charge. "Miss Diesha told us that to get the engagement sticker, we have to do something above and beyond collecting data. So let's each pick a different topic and learn everything about it we can."

This seemed like a pretty good plan. So we divided up to look for information on different pigeon-related topics. This time, I asked Jasmine to work with me before Ivy could get to her. Ivy looked disappointed, but within minutes, she was off with Erica. Soon our table was piled high with books. We dug into them, searching for ideas. Miss Diesha would be so impressed.

Erica said she wanted to compare pigeons' social lives to those of humans. When she announced this idea, Pablo said, "Yeah, because we all act so much like pigeons." And that's when it started:

Neeko shouted: "I'm a pigeon, I'm a pigeon! Follow me!" He strutted around between the aisles of books, bobbing his head.

Pablo laughed and followed.

Ivy: "Look, Neeko's being courted. He's found his mate!"

Everyone went crazy, acting like pigeons bobbing their heads, running around in circles, and making pigeon noises. Neeko jumped up on a chair, flapping his arms like wings. I stood to the side, watching. It was a crazy

sight! Then Erica and Ivy collided. You could hear the sound of their skulls knocking together. They had to sit on the floor. Erica was howling about it when the librarian appeared.

At first, no one noticed her. But then she clapped her hands and said "Hey!" real loud. When she had our attention, she reminded us of the rules of the library and warned us that if she had to come over again, she'd alert security, and we'd be kicked out.

Neeko bobbed his head as the librarian walked away, and the girls tried to hold in their giggles.

Pablo said to me: "I'm going to do research on why pigeons bob their heads."

Me: "I was wondering about that too."

Pablo: "You, um, want to work on it together?"

I was glad he asking me, but instead of saying yes, I thought about my upcoming doctor's appointment and how I didn't know what was going to happen. What if I end up in the hospital in some sort of leg-straightening contraption, or have to have surgery? I don't want to be a bad partner and leave him in the lurch, so I said, "No thanks."

His face fell, so I quickly added, "But want to trade some comics? Just to read, I mean. The best DC you have for my best Marvel? Or I have issues of *The Tick*."

Guess what? He said yes!

And—even better—he has some old *Tick* cartoons from the '90s on DVD that he's going to lend me.

Legs

Mom is letting me stay home from school today. My legs hurt so much that I was up all night, and there was no hiding it from her. Plus, on top of my leg pain, I'm running a fever, and my stomach hurts. Mom doesn't have to work until this afternoon, so she's been making me hot chocolate and toast with butter, fluffing my pillow, and patting my cheeks. She's the best.

In a panic, I realized that TJ and I were supposed to meet after school today. Mom offered to call TJ to cancel, but I knew I'd never hear the end of it if "Mommy" called, so I picked up my phone. I barely got it out when someone started yelling at him in the background. He hung up quick, before I could ask him to go on his own.

This is lame. How are TJ and I ever going to catch up? No way is he going to get out here and collect data without me. I can't believe my fate of going to the museum is in his hands! I can feel that fieldwork sticker slipping away. And what about my presentation? That's coming up soon, but I can't prep if I'm lying here. I don't even have a topic picked out yet. I'll never earn the Data Collection badge or get to go on the museum overnight. Why did I join, anyway?

Later, I heard Mom on the phone with the doctor's office, telling them I am in really rough shape and asking for a sooner appointment.

A marathon of classic cartoons couldn't make me feel better. Neither could listening to a playlist of the most upbeat music I could find.

I got to sleep some. My fever broke, and I'm feeling a little better now.

Mom had to leave for work, but she had Mr. Geo stop by to keep an eye on me. Which was annoying. I stay home alone when I'm not sick, so why can't I now?

But him coming by ended up being a good thing. He brought me some really tasty chicken soup along with the kind of crackers I like. And he gave me this really cool comic book catalog that has pages of cover art and summaries of the series—great for scoping out the competition. Sometimes he's really not so bad.

Jasmine came by too. I asked her to check up on Scrapper to make sure he's okay. He's used to me coming around and probably misses the snacks. She said she would and offered to help me collect pigeon data after I felt better.

When I said no thanks, and wouldn't that be unfair to Ivy, she said that it was Ivy's idea in the first place!

That surprised me. And made me feel like I should try to be a little nicer to Ivy.

The Dreaded Doctor's Appointment

BAD news!!

I missed school again today, this time because of a doctor's appointment. I HATE going to the doctor's. And it took ALL day. The fact that Mom had been able to move up the appointment, which originally was supposed to be a month from now, felt like a red flag. She must think it's serious.

Dr. Khan has a roll-y, sing-y way of talking that relaxes me. He could make sentences like "Without proper treatment you have only thirty days to live" sound like a gentle song. His voice could seriously lull me to sleep.

It was such a relief when he took off my braces. They pinch and rub so much now I can barely fit into them. Dr. Khan said we could make some adjustments before I left. He felt up and down my legs. "Hmm, hmm" he muttered. His hands were cool, and since he was bent over, I could see the bald spot on the top of his head. I focused my stare there, a hairless island in a hairy sea.

He stood up, his eyes big and brown like a puppy dog's. "I'd like an X-ray of both legs, then we'll discuss the results."

Grrr. More waiting, this time in an embarrassing white-and-blue printed hospital gown that tied in the back and would have fit someone three times my size.

The technician was really nice, even though he almost crushed me when he draped this heavy lead cape over my torso to protect the rest of me from the X-rays.

Then more endless waiting for the doctor to look at the X-rays and see us again. Mom rubbed her hands a lot and tried to say positive things like, "At least we'll get answers today," and "This will all be fine, wait and see." I stayed pretty quiet because I was hungry, tired, and uncomfortable, and I didn't want to take it out on her.

Finally, we got to see Dr. Khan again. "It is the Blount's disease that is causing you pain. Your shin bones are growing too fast again, and this time, surgery will be necessary."

I asked what would happen if I didn't have surgery. He told me that my symptoms would slowly get worse. My legs would bow a lot and could eventually make me unable to walk without braces. My ears started to buzz. I did NOT want anyone cutting into me, taking out part of my body. And I also did not want to end up in a wheelchair. I have been waiting for the day I can get my leg braces off and play basketball with the other guys.

Dr. Khan must have read my face, because he said that the surgery is small, and compared to the rest of my life, the recovery time is short. He plans to restrict the growth of the outer half of the shin bone so my natural growth on the other side will balance things out. He told us this condition is most common among early walkers (me! I started walking at nine months), the obese (*not* me!), and black children (me again). When it's all done, he said my legs will look normal. In the meantime, I should try to keep busy to distract myself from when they hurt.

Whatever he did to my leg braces, they feel better now. Walking out of the hospital, my legs barely hurt. It made me feel hopeful.

When we got home, Mr. Geo was there, and he had brought dinner for a change, instead of eating ours.

Sports Announcer

Jasmine came by over the weekend to bring me my homework so I could catch up.

She also brought me a pile of comics from Pablo and said he had asked how I was doing. This made me happy. She had other good news too: She said that TJ brought in data to the Science Squad meeting I missed. So at least he's trying.

I was feeling restless, so we walked down to the park. Jasmine is always real nice about pretending that I don't slow her down. I was walking funnier than usual. Even with the braces, trying get around hurt with each step.

Scrapper wasn't there, but then again, it was much earlier than usual. Even Mr. Garamelli hadn't showed up yet. I didn't worry—both Scrapper and Mr. G would both probably show up later, at the usual time.

Unlike TJ, Jas is a pro at telling the different color morphs apart. In no time, she had helped me collect a couple of pages of good, solid data. A bunch of people were eating breakfast bagels and pastries, so there were more pigeons than ever.

They were all crowding around the benches, jockeying for crumbs. Jasmine laughed, and after we were done counting, she pretended she was a sports commentator: "It's a tight competition, folks, the red-bar is up three bits of bagel. But here comes a blue-bar, driving up on the left, jockeying for position . . . and there you have it, folks, he's just scored the prize chunk of donut!"

I have to admit, they can be funny to watch.

Later, The Mouth and I lounged on our beds and read the comics from Pablo—mostly *Justice League*. DC comics are really not all that bad. They gave me some great ideas for my Dino Tech Destroyers comic. For example, I've decided I need a lead human character. And he'll have an animal sidekick, kind of like me and Scrapper.

I wonder what Pablo would think of my idea?

Back at School

Today, I suited up my leg braces and headed to school.

Knowing I was going to have surgery soon made everything look a little different. Like it wasn't as big or as important as it had been before. If TJ made fun of me, I was pretty sure I wouldn't even care.

It didn't take long to test that theory. We weren't even through first period when Mrs. Coleman called on me for the answer to a math problem. It was a tough one, and I got it right. TJ jumped in to say, quietly enough so Mrs. Coleman couldn't hear, "Pidge getting a right answer? But that doesn't add up."

This time, I didn't pull up my hood or look down at my notebook or try to make myself invisible like I usually do. Instead, I looked right at him.

Our eyes locked.

I stared him down. A hard stare. I channeled steel and fire.

He stared back but then looked away.

Thanks to my finely honed powers of observation, it was now crystal clear that every time I say something smart, TJ makes a comment to cut me down. He's lashing out, but really it has nothing to do with me. It's all about him. Like Mr. Garamelli kicking the pigeon. Just realizing this makes me feel better. It's like I had been wearing one of those heavy X-ray protector aprons all the time and finally figured out how to slip out from under it.

I felt so light that I smiled at Erica and even Ivy. At lunch, I heard Erica say to Jasmine, "Anthony's cool. Ask him to sit with us if you want."

She called me ANTHONY. Whoa.

That was enough for me to forget about the ache in my legs for all of English class. I decided I would make those girls a poster that rocks. I spent a lot of class secretly laying out what I want it to look like in my notebook.

When I saw Pablo, I thanked him for comics and pulled out some issues of The Tick that I had put in my backpack just for him.

At dinner, The Mouth kept eyeing me. I knew he wanted to know why I was smiling so much, especially since I'm going to have surgery soon, but I just gave him a big grin and offered him the biggest slice of pizza on the plate. Sometimes it's nice to keep a little something to yourself.

Enter Falcon

I finally made it back to the park today. I looked around for Scrapper but didn't see him. Mr. Garamelli called me over.

Mr. Garamelli: "You're just in time. Look up." He pointed out a big bird high in the sky. "Do you know what that is?"

Me: "A falcon?"

Mr. Garamelli: "Yes, and not just any falcon—it's a peregrine, the fastest animal on Earth. I thought you might be interested, since peregrine falcons eat pigeons."

At first, I was my old pigeon-hating self. I was like, *YES! Yes! This is what I'll do my presentation on! A fast and ferocious predator.* Then I thought about Scrapper. Let's face it, he's a little slower than the other pigeons. An easy catch. Suddenly I didn't like the way that falcon was hanging around. I hoped Scrapper was roosting somewhere out of sight, safe and sound. I did NOT want him to become a falcon snack.

Mr. Garamelli and I were talking when TJ showed up. He hung back at first, but when he heard that we were talking about falcons, he came closer. Mr. Garamelli said there are a lot here in New York. Just like the pigeons, they like the habitat that the tall buildings provide. And cities often have plenty of food for them too—in the form of pigeons.

Me: "Sounds like peregrine falcons could be a good project for the engagement sticker." If I learned more about them, maybe I could also figure out a way to protect Scrapper.

TJ: "Hmm."

Hmm? Now I wish I had asked TJ what he meant by that. Is he planning to do HIS presentation on falcons? Because that's what I think I want to do!

Still No Scrapper

I'm feeling more and more anxious about Scrapper. It's all I can think about. He wasn't there again today, even though I waited in the park for hours. Mr. Garamelli hadn't seen him either, which says a lot, considering how much time he spends there.

And we saw the falcon again, this time perched on the ledge of a nearby building. The falcon spread his wings and launched into the air, and a thin spread of panic started in my chest and radiated out to my arms and legs. Every bit of me was tingling. He was hunting! I needed to get out of the park and do something. I needed to understand falcons and what they do, and whether the falcon's presence had anything to do with Scrapper's absence.

TJ, late as usual, was on his way into the park as I headed out.

TJ: "Hey! Where you going? Slow down!"

Me: "Library. Going to research falcons. Come or not, I don't care."

He followed. Once there, we pulled out every book on falcons we could find. TJ was pretty into it. I still don't trust the guy, but he did find a bunch of facts to help me put together this falcon fact list:

- Falcons soar through the air at speeds of up to 240 miles per hour, and they can dive even faster than they can fly.
- They grab pigeons in flight with their sharp talons.
- A falcon may kill one or two pigeons a day.
- Pigeons may make up seventy-five percent of their diet.
- Falcons often chase the weaker members of a group.

I was getting more and more nervous, even though we found these facts too:

- Pigeons learn where falcons nest and stay away.
- Pigeons can easily reach fifty to sixty miles per hour. They can fly as high as six thousand feet.
- Pigeons often know to fly higher than a falcon so the falcon can't dive at them.
- Pigeons will twist and turn in the air to avoid being nabbed.

- *And pigeons can fly for a long time without getting tired. They can go as far as six hundred miles in a day.*

Now, every time I closed my eyes, I could see the falcon dive-bombing Scrapper, his massive claws extended, closing in around Scrapper's little body even as he tries to shift out of the way on his stiff leg.

My chest got so tight it was hard to breathe. If Scrapper can't survive, how can I? Darwin wrote about survival of the fittest, which means the strongest, fastest, and smartest are most likely to survive. Why does it have to be that way? What about survival of the nicest or the most earnest?

Then I did the worst thing I could ever do in front of TJ.

I cried.

At Home, Upset

I bolted out of there as fast as I could go, but I know TJ saw. When I think about school tomorrow, my stomach squeezes tight. I'll have a new nickname, even worse than before: Pouty Pidge. Or maybe it'll be Pidge the Crybaby, or Bawling Ball of Bird Feathers.

Thinking of names, I almost make myself laugh. Key word: almost.

I'm spending the entire night in my room. No way am I going out into the kitchen where I'll have to talk to everyone. Mr. Geo is out there—I can hear his voice. I can also smell sausage jambalaya being reheated. Even though this is one of my all-time favorites that Mom barely ever brings home, and even though she's asked me to come out and join them three times already, I'm staying put. I told her I'm just really, really tired and need to rest. Thankfully, she didn't pry with a lot of questions like she sometimes does.

A little while ago, The Mouth came in and asked me if everything was okay. I told him no, it wasn't. I know he thought I was talking about my legs because he said, "It's not going to be like this forever." But if Scrapper got eaten by a falcon, it would be *forever. Nothing can change that. But I didn't bother to correct The Mouth . . . what's the point? He told me to go ahead and look through his vintage Hot Wheels car collection (he never does anything with it, but usually he won't let me touch it), so I know he felt sorry for me. That made me feel both better and even worse.*

After he went back out to eat, I put on a playlist of electronic music that suited my mood: dark and moody. I listened until the room turned dark. Then, when the apartment fell quiet, I slipped out into the bathroom to brush my teeth and wash my face. Then back to bed. When Mom came in to check on me, I breathed slow and deep so she'd think I was asleep. I did the same thing when The Mouth came in to go to sleep. No way did I want to talk to anyone.

Now he's snoring, so my nightlight is on, and I'm back to writing and drawing. I came up with another comic idea:

A giant, evil T. rex is about to grab a pterodactyl out of the sky. The pterodactyl would be a goner, but the human hero (who happens to look a lot like me) steps in just in time. Even though the T. rex could snap him in half like a toothpick, the hero manages to distract the T. rex long enough so the pterodactyl can get away.

Can You Believe It?

Can you believe, TJ did not mention me crying to anyone at school!?!?!?! A year ago, it would have been all he could talk about!

I was sitting in first period when TJ walked in. I could feel myself stiffen up. I looked straight ahead, bracing myself for whatever was going to come out of his mouth.

But all he did was walk by, giving my desk a couple of raps with his knuckles as he passed.

Huh? What did he mean by that? Was it a friendly, "Hey Bud," or a warning, "Watch out because I have knowledge that can utterly humiliate you"?

Now it's almost the end of the school day (I'm writing this during English, since I'm ahead on the classwork), and TJ has yet to say anything. Still, I need to stay on guard. It doesn't mean he won't cut me down with it the next time I say something smart. Clearly, it's time to go back to being more invisible again.

I couldn't focus on anything today. Everyone around me seemed to be on a different planet. They were laughing and talking about the Squad and homework—things that didn't feel important to me anymore. It was like I had stepped into a sludge of gray loneliness and was sinking deeper and deeper as each class passed.

No one else can feel the pain in my legs or the heavy weight pressing on my chest when I think about Scrapper. It makes me wonder what kind of private feelings other people are carrying around. Like TJ and his family problems. But still, it's not okay for him to use me as a scapegoat for his feelings.

I looked at him, as if my powers of observation would suddenly give me a clue, and he glanced over at me. Our eyes met, and this time, I didn't see meanness or anger in them, just curiosity. We both looked away, but it felt different, like we'd reached an understanding.

At lunch, Pablo tried to talk to me about a new comic release he was excited about, but I couldn't get into it. The conversation just kind of fizzled out. And then I felt bad about that too because I've started to think Pablo is a pretty interesting guy and want to get to know him better.

Of course Jasmine noticed my mood, so I told her about the falcon and that Scrapper was missing (but left out the crying part).

Jasmine: "I think we should announce it at the Squad meeting today and get everyone to look. Like a search and rescue."

Me: "They won't. Why would they?"

Jasmine, huffing in frustration: "Anthony!! The real question is, why WOULDNT they?"

That got me thinking. The girls had asked me to make them a poster. Neeko had joked with me when we entered data at the Squad meeting. And Pablo had asked me to work on the engagement sticker with him. I felt a spark of hope. Maybe they did like me enough to help. And with everyone looking, there'd be a much better chance of finding Scrapper.

All at once, I felt excited, anxious, and nervous. I got to work on a notebook-sized poster of Scrapper, showing his splashes of white and the funny-shaped spot on his head. I worked on it through the next three classes, right through to just a few minutes ago. Now I'm done, waiting for the meeting and wondering if I have the nerve to go through with this.

A Call for Help!

At the Squad meeting, Jasmine whispered, "Do it!" And gave me a little shove. For all her love of animals, that girl doesn't mind pushing me around.

I took a deep breath and asked Miss Diesha if I could say something. Then I turned to face the group. I showed the poster and told the story of Scrapper. At one point, I got choked up. But I pushed on.

"So I'm asking for your help to find Scrapper."

The room was completely quiet. So quiet, I could hear the clock ticking on the wall.

Tick, tock. Tick, tock.

I waited for the laughter, and the catcall from TJ. But it didn't come.

Something was thumping pretty loudly in my ears. It was my heart! My eyes blurred with tears as I looked out into the sea of faces in front of me. I shouldn't have asked. I needed to get out of there.

"I'll help," TJ said loudly, raising his hand.

What?! My knees almost buckled in surprise. "Me too," said Jasmine. All the girls agreed. Pablo's and everyone else's hands went up.

TJ: "Pigeon hunting par-tay!"

For once, his stupid comment didn't annoy me.

Miss Diesha clapped her hands together. "I think this Squad has a mission. Let's all head to the park where Anthony last saw Scrapper. We'll put our observation skills to the test and see what clues we can find."

I couldn't believe it. A wave of relief almost keeled me over—and almost pushed more tears out of my eyes.

Within fifteen minutes, we all flooded into the park. Neeko got there last—he'd gotten a big bag of the seed mix to feed the pigeons. We passed it around, and everyone took a handful. Soon we had flocks of pigeons swarming around us.

Of course Mr. Garamelli was curious about all the kids and action in *his* park. He came over and struck up a conversion with Miss Diesha, who explained the situation. I wanted to tell them, "Stop talking and start looking!"

I scanned the birds over and over, looking for Scrapper's telltale white markings.

Ivy called out to say she thought she found him. I came rushing over, but it was a different pigeon with a bum leg. It turns out that pigeons with injured or missing feet are not all that uncommon. It's a tough life on the city streets.

Then Neeko thought he saw Scrapper because a bird had a white blotch on its neck, but I could tell right away it wasn't. Funny, a couple of months ago, I didn't know the difference between a pied and a blue-bar, but now I could pick Scrapper out of a lineup of ten similar-looking birds.

Even though we hadn't found Scrapper, my spirits were lifting because:

- I was taking action.
- My Squad members were helping me.
- I could feel how much they really wanted to help.

I looked around and saw that every one of my fellow Squad members was looking— even TJ. My legs and arms tingled, but this time it wasn't from anxiety. It was from knowing that I was on the inside of something instead of the outside. They were all helping me, ME.

Everyone put in a good effort, but Scrapper just wasn't there. We didn't see any evidence of the falcon either (because he was probably back at home on his nest, feeding filleted pigeon delight to his chicks).

We were about to call it quits when Mr. Garamelli had an idea.

As they say at the end of a comic, "To be continued . . ."

(I need to shake out my hand, get a snack, and then get in the mood to write the rest by picking out some suspenseful music.)

A Call for Help, Part 2

(Suspenseful music now playing)

Mr. Garamelli said that he lives in an apartment building across from the park. (So he does have a place to live!) He said that lately, there have been a lot of pigeon sounds coming from just outside his kitchen window, but he hadn't bothered to see who was making them.

"Maybe your pigeon friend has been hanging out up there. Pigeons love that building. If you step out into my courtyard, you'll see more hanging around some of the other apartments too."

I looked at Miss Diesha. She smiled. "It's a long shot, but we might as well give it a try," she said.

The next thing I knew, we were ALL streaming down the sidewalk to Mr. Garamelli's apartment building, Neeko and TJ in the lead. Before long, my legs were on fire, and I was falling behind. Miss Diesha kept in step with me. When we finally got to the building, everyone stopped and caught their breath while we waited for Mr. Garamelli, who brought up the tail end.

He eyed the crowd in front of his building. "The courtyard is a small place, and I don't want to overwhelm the other tenants—so let's have just two kids at a time, plus Miss Diesha. Anthony, you first."

I pointed to Jasmine. "Her too." He raised his eyebrows at me, then winked and smiled. I could feel myself get hot.

The courtyard was small and cozy. Grapevines crept up the brick walls, and small plots of plants made interesting patterns around a narrow gravel path. I'll bet it looks nice and lush when everything leafs out in the spring. A long, wide wooden bench was tucked against one wall. We followed the path to two white metal chairs and a matching metal table. I wondered if Mr. Garamelli ever came out to sit here too. Then we looked up and scanned the windowsills and balconies that lined the inner walls of the building. Pigeon poop streaked the sills and the brick just below them, but there were no pigeons in sight. I could feel my mood about to go into a free fall.

"What about up there?" asked Jasmine.

On a ledge just overhead was a nest—with a pigeon on it!! But it was a red-bar, not Scrapper.

Together, Miss Diesha, Jasmine, and I dragged the wooden bench close (but not too close) and climbed on top for a better view. We watched the pigeon move around. I couldn't see, but it looked like something else was in the nest too. Eggs?

Then, out of the corner of my eye, I spotted something flying toward the nest. IT WAS SCRAPPER!

We watched as Scrapper landed on the edge of the nest. The red-bar moved to make room, revealing two gray-white babies!! Scrapper was a parent!

I squeezed Jasmine's arm, and she squeezed mine. Scrapper wasn't falcon food after all!!

"Well, well, well," said Mr. Garamelli.

Miss Diesha said, "Pigeon chicks! Now this is a rare sight! Pigeons are very good at hiding their nests. And the baby pigeons—which are called squabs—remain in the nest until they look like adults. Humans usually don't get to see them."

Other kids took turns coming in and out to have a look. I just stayed there, grinning from ear to ear, watching Scrapper snuggle in with his chicks.

My legs could have caught fire, and I wouldn't have noticed.

Squab Watching

I have a new routine. Every day after collecting pigeon data, I head over to Mr. Garamelli's courtyard. Different kids come along each day. Sometimes it's Jasmine, sometimes it's Ivy, Pablo, or even TJ. While Mr. Garamelli sits at the little metal table and reads, we hang out, watching Scrapper and his mate take care of their squabs.

It's really interesting. The nest is made of small twigs. Scrapper and his mate both provide for their chicks, which are growing bigger and bigger right before my eyes. They're ugly-cute, just like the frogmouth bird on Jas's T-shirt. I've been turning on my powers of observation full blast when I'm at the nest, and I'm pretty sure I can already tell the two babies apart. One has darker gray skin around its eyes than the other.

Baby pigeons, once they leave their protected nests at about eight weeks, look almost exactly like adult pigeons. Here's how to tell a young pigeon from a full adult: Adult pigeons have orange or red-orange eyes. Young pigeons under eight months old have brown or gray-brown eyes. Also, the cere, the fleshy covering on the upper part of a pigeon's beak, is white on adult pigeons but gray on young pigeons.

And even though my legs are always throbbing now, and I'm scheduled to have surgery in a little over a week, today was an awesome standout day. The best thing ever happened, and in front of Pablo too: Scrapper flew over to the balcony. I took some of the seeds I brought with me and dropped a few on my shoe. I held my hand, which also had seeds in it, close by, just like I used to do at the park. And guess what? Scrapper came right over—and for the first time, he ate straight out of my hand.

His pecks felt hard and ticklish at the same time, and I had to work to keep from laughing and pulling my hand away.

Pablo: "I can't believe that just happened. It's like you have pigeon superpowers!"

That got us to talking about why pigeons are like superheroes. Here's our list:

- *Pigeons have an amazing sense of sight, way better than any human's.*
- *Same thing for hearing. They can hear sounds that are way lower than anything we can.*
- *They can fly long distances.*
- *They are excellent navigators.*

Pablo also agreed to help me with Dino Tech Destroyers, as a colorist. Plus, he told me that pigeons are descended from dinosaurs, just like sea turtles. How cool is that? I've got to work that into my cartoon.

Plus, now I know what I am going to do my Science Squad presentation on.

Data Crunching

The time's gone by fast, watching the squabs.

Luckily, we are analyzing our data and presenting our projects *before* I have to miss a bunch of school for surgery. It's so perfectly timed that I half wonder if Miss Diesha moved up the dates just to make sure I could be included.

Once everyone entered all their data into the Science Squad website, it was obvious that TJ and I didn't get as much data as everyone else. I was freaking out inside over not getting a fieldwork sticker, when Ivy made this announcement:

"I really think we should all combine our data efforts. Like Miss Diesha said, it's about the team, getting curious, and expanding our knowledge through work and perseverance. I think that as a Squad, we've done all that."

Everyone cheered!

That was very generous of her to say, since she and Jasmine collected the most of everyone. At that moment, I could see why Jasmine really likes her.

Miss Diesha said that she agreed, everyone had put in great effort and deserved a sticker. She said that in science, it's not about quantity of data, but quality, and that collecting data from a place that has less pigeons can be just as meaningful as collecting from a crowded place.

Ivy wanted to show data visually, so she made a pie chart of the percentages of each color morph—it turns out that for our area, blue-bars and checkers are most common. But these percentages vary in other places.

After that, we all looked at our data for other patterns. But as hard as we tried, we couldn't find any clear patterns that would help us figure out why pigeons come in so many different morphs. We kept looking because we didn't want to disappoint Miss Diesha.

Erica: "At least we can say that they don't choose mates based on feather color. Look, there's no pattern to how the different color morphs pair up to mate."

She was right; we were able to eliminate that one hypothesis. But that was it. We took what we'd found to

Miss Diesha. We thought she'd be disappointed, but here's what she said:

"I am so glad the project is working out this way. The Science Squad motto is to 'Ask questions, seek answers.' That doesn't mean we'll get nice, clean-cut answers—not right away, anyway. This reflects real science. Data can be messy and unclear, especially at first. I hope you carry this truth about science with you as you continue to grow as scientists, and as people who read about science in the news."

Now that is interesting! I always thought science was black-and-white. But it makes sense that as you observe more and more and notice more things, you can ask better and better questions. For example, if I hadn't noticed Pablo hiding comics in his notebook, I could only have asked him a general question, like "What do you like to read?" But now that I've observed him reading comics, I know I can ask him a more specific question, like "Which issues of *The Tick* are your favorite?"

The more you know, the more you know what to ask.

But back to Miss Diesha, the Squad, and some of the ideas we talked about.

Miss Diesha: "A hypothesis I personally want to test is that maybe there are more dark birds up north than light birds, since dark colors absorb more heat and could help keep them warm. Any ideas on how to test this?"

Ivy: "You could compare how many dark and light birds there are in a northern place, like New York or Maine, to a southern place, like Florida?"

Miss Diesha: "That would certainly bring me closer to an answer."

Neeko: "I was talking to my brother, and he said different color morphs are constantly escaping from people's coops. So I'm thinking that if those birds get out there and join up with all the wild city pigeons, that helps keep the color diversity up."

Miss Diesha: "Excellent! That is a very possible explanation."

Pablo: "Or maybe there just aren't many predators here in NYC to attack and eat the colorful or odd-colored birds. So all the different colored birds survive and mate and pass all the different colors on to their babies."

We all kept throwing out more ideas, hypotheses, and questions for the next hour. It's a good thing the Squad

is going to keep working on the Project Pigeon Power,
even after we earn our engagement stickers. There's
more data to collect, and more hypotheses to test!

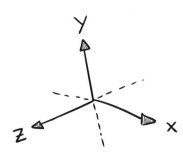

The Engagement Sticker

Today everyone in the Squad gave our presentations . . . and they all rocked. Here's a list of a few of the highlights:

• **TJ**: Kicked butt using the falcon info we collected at the library. (Yeah, I let him use it once I decided to present another topic.)

• **Neeko**: Invited us all on a field trip next week for a demo on pigeon racing. (Drat—I'm going to miss it!) Then he told a story about the bus garage his dad worked at, and how it had a problem with too many pigeons hanging out in the bay. So one day, Neeko's dad and another worker caught them all in a great big net, boxed them up, and drove them far, far away—hundreds of miles—before letting them go. By the time they got back to the garage . . . the pigeons were there, waiting for them! Turns out, pigeons have amazing navigation skills and can always find their way home.

• **Pablo**: *Told us that pigeons' breast muscles, which are used for flight, take up one-third of their total body weight, and racing pigeons can fly up to 110 miles per hour. That's faster than I've ever gone in any kind of vehicle! Pablo also told us that Mike Tyson (the famous boxer) loves to raise and race pigeons—and is known to kiss them. So maybe Neeko's not alone after all . . .*

• **Jasmine and Ivy**: *Did a joint presentation. Before, I would have felt a pang of jealous badness over this, but now I just sat back and enjoyed their top-notch presentation on experiments people have done with pigeons to demonstrate their smarts. They told us about how pigeons can do math. Scientists have done experiments to show that pigeons can tell the difference between groups with different numbers of objects in them and put them in order, from lowest to highest. Besides humans, monkeys are the only other animal known to be able to do this.*

Pigeons keep impressing scientists with their many skills and smarts. Researchers have recently found that pigeons can learn to put everyday things into categories. They do this by figuring out which details are important and which aren't, just like humans do. In one study, pigeons put 128 photos of objects into sixteen categories, such as baby, car, cracker, dog, fish, flower, key, and shoe. They learned to place objects they had never seen before into the correct category.

When it was my turn, I put on some epic-style background music.

I made a slideshow with tons of images of Scrapper, his mate, and the squabs. Mr. Garamelli let me use his fancy digital camera to take them. I swear Scrapper let me get close because he recognizes me. For real! Pigeons are smart like that.

I talked about how private nesting pigeons are, how they mate for life, how they co-parent. Pigeons usually lay two white eggs, which take about eighteen days to hatch. Both the male and female take turns sitting on the eggs, and both make a Jell-O-like baby food, called pigeon or crop milk, to feed the squabs. And I shared some of my private observations, such as that even when Scrapper isn't feeding the babies, he hangs out nearby, as if he is protecting them. And the way he coos and struts on the ledge near the nest, he seems happy and proud.

I finished with not one rude or snide question or comment from TJ. He asked if any other birds feed their young crop milk—a real question! (As far as I know, only pigeons, flamingos, and one kind of penguin do this.)

Mr. Mitts, Ms. Michaelson, and all our other teachers were there. Afterward, Ms. Michaelson suggested I write up my story and send it to *Kids National Geographic* with the photos, which she said are rare and special.

And then . . . Miss Diesha presented me with the engagement sticker!

Miss Diesha: "Anthony, this is for all the excellent observations you've made about Scrapper and his family. And for your persistence and teamwork. You truly have gone above and beyond on this Squad. This is exactly what I meant by going the extra mile!"

And guess what, everyone started cheering and chanting, "Pidge, Pidge, Pidge!"

I guess it's not such a bad nickname after all.

Surgery

I finally got that poster for the sixth grade neighborhood fundraiser done. I wouldn't want to keep Erica and her gang waiting. They seemed really happy with what I gave them.

It's a good thing too, since my first surgery is tomorrow. It'll be on my left leg. A few months later, they'll fix my right. After each operation, I'm going to wear a special, extra heavy-duty brace around that leg to guide the growth of my shinbone for a few weeks. Then, once that's off, I'll have to use crutches for a while. Also, I'll have to have physical therapy sessions twice a week to learn exercises to help make my leg healthy and strong. The Mouth has already volunteered to take me. The doctor told me once I build up my leg strength, I'll be able to walk normally and can start playing sports if I want. I can't wait!

Most important of all, even though I've earned all the stickers I need for the Data Collection badge, the museum overnight isn't until late spring. That's months away. That means I'll have plenty of time to recover from my surgery before it's time. Good thing, because I am seriously looking forward to it. Pablo and I have agreed to set up our sleeping bags next to each other, and the four of us—Jasmine, Ivy, Pablo, and me—have plans to spend at least some of the time in the Hall of New York City Birds. And of course, Pablo and I are going to scope out as many of the dinosaurs as possible.

In the meantime, Jasmine, TJ, and Pablo have all said they'll keep an eye on Scrapper while I'm getting better from the surgery, until I can make it back up to Mr. Garamelli's apartment. Who knows? By then, maybe the squabs will be old enough to leave the nest, and Scrapper will be back down in the park.

Which reminds me, I have the ending of my Dino Tech Destroyers comic figured out: Two heroes (who look like Pablo and me) spot a pterodactyl (that has a white spot on its head) circling overhead. It shows them the way to the portal back to the dino world. Each hero rides a speedy Allosaurus, and together, they capture the whole army of meat-eaters, handcuffing the dinos together by their teeny-tiny front legs. They make the dinos march back through the portal, and Earth is saved!

(Time to blast some seriously epic, pounding, dance-'til-you-drop African drumming and start drawing!)

Fact File

The Who: Pigeons, also known as Rock Pigeons or Rock Doves (scientific name: *Columba livia*), are so common that they practically blend in to the background, especially in cities. Maybe that's why scientists know less about them than many other birds.

The What: The Pigeon Watch Project, which the fictional Project Pigeon Power in this book was modeled after, was a citizen science research project headed by the Cornell Lab of Ornithology in Ithaca, New York. Its purpose was to figure out why city pigeons come in so many colors and whether they choose their mates based on color.

The How: Citizen scientists were asked to gather data for the project by counting how many pigeons of each color were in different flocks and marking down which colors mated with which.

The Where: Cornell scientists recruited kid and adult volunteers in ten different countries, including Canada, Mexico, Japan, Greece, Russia, and the United States.

The Why: Pigeons are the only kind of bird that exists in a whole bunch of different colors. This diversity came about when wild blue-bar Rock Pigeons were domesticated and bred to have many different feather patterns. But when these birds returned to the wild, the next generations didn't go back to having a more uniform blue-bar pattern. This is very unusual, and to this day, scientists still haven't figured out exactly why they have kept such a remarkable number of color patterns.

The When: The Pigeon Watch Project ran from 1998 until 2007, at which point it was merged into a new citizen science project called Celebrate Urban Birds. This project focuses on sixteen species of birds found in cities and looks at how they interact with urban green spaces.

 # In the Field

Urban areas aren't usually considered to be birdwatching hot spots, but Karen Purcell, former project leader of the Pigeon Watch Project, says that city pigeons are so common, they often get overlooked. Yet these incredibly intelligent birds have many cool and interesting behaviors. The Pigeon Watch Project inspired many kids and adults alike to learn more about them.

Today, Purcell is the project leader for Celebrate Urban Birds, another citizen science project that studies the birds that live in, or migrate through, cities and surrounding areas. The goal of the project is to better understand their needs, especially when it comes to green spaces like parks, trees, or even balcony gardens.

But science can be unpredictable. Scientists often begin collecting data to answer a question, but that doesn't mean they will get an answer. According to Purcell, "science is messy. You get information, learn a little, then maybe ask a different question." Through this process, she explains, "slowly you get closer to the truth."

Glossary

bachata — A style of music and dance that originated in the Dominican Republic and features guitars and percussion.

bars — Wide lines of color on a bird's wing.

billing — When a female bird puts her bill inside a male's when they are courting.

cere — The fleshy area just above the beak of some birds.

checkered — A feather color pattern where the pigeon's wings have alternating areas of different colors.

courting — Behavior that is meant to attract a mate.

dovecote — A small house or box where domestic pigeons live.

guano — The waste of birds and bats.

morph — One form of a physical feature, such as a color or pattern.

ornithology — The scientific study of birds.

pied — A feather color pattern where the pigeon has spots or patches of white feathers on its body or wings.

pigeon milk — A special substance rich in protein and fat, made by adult pigeons to feed their babies.

squab — A young pigeon, one to thirty days old.

Selected Bibliography

Blechman, Andrew D. *Pigeons: The Fascinating Saga of the World's Most Revered and Reviled Bird.* New York: Grove Press, 2006.

"Rock Pigeon." *Celebrate Urban Birds.* https://celebrateurbanbirds.org/learn/birds/focal-species/rock-pigeon/. Accessed February 21, 2018.

"Rock Pigeon Identification." *The Cornell Lab of Ornithology.* https://www.allaboutbirds.org/guide/Rock_Pigeon/id. Accessed February 21, 2018.

About the Author

Jodie Mangor is a science and children's writer. When she's not writing books for kids, she puts her degrees in microbiology, environmental science, and molecular biology to work developing grant proposals for all sorts of cool new science inventions. She is also the author of audio tour scripts for high-profile museums and tourist destinations (like the Statue of Liberty!) around the world. Many of these tours are for kids. She lives in Ithaca, New York, with her family.

About the Illustrator

Arpad Olbey is an illustrator veteran and art director of his art studio in London. He works with paper, pencils, and paints, or digital high-tech equipment, depending on the project. His wish is to combine his experience and technical knowledge to deliver the best that his creativity can give to audiences.

Explore Even More
SCIENCE SQUAD!

by J. A. Watson   Illustrated by Arpad Olbey

AVAILABLE NOW!